'He's never wanted anything but this. If he loses, he might as well be dead.'

It's an opportunity a journalist and ex-boxer with a complicated personal life can't turn down: joining the camp of the world title challenger, Ricky Mallon, in the lead-up to the championship fight. For Billy Piers it's more than work, its an escape route from Karen, loving and beautiful but disturbed, and unaware of what he's going through – that he's in love with someone else, someone who can't decide who she is in love with at all.

THE CHAMPION'S NEW CLOTHES is about love and old friendships, and about loneliness and violence, from the brutality of the boxing ring to the cruelty that goes hand in hand with love. As Ricky trains for the biggest fight of his life, Billy faces the hardest decision of his. Both men are fuelled by desire, and both come to learn that nothing is ever what it seems and that it is desire itself which creates the cruellest illusions of all. With wit and acute honesty, THE CHAMPION'S NEW CLOTHES warns: Beware of what you want. You might get it.

THE CHAMPION'S NEW CLOTHES

THE CHAMPION'S NEW CLOTHES

Barry Graham

BLOOMSBURY

First published in Great Britain 1991

Bloomsbury Publishing Ltd, 2 Soho Square, London W1V 5DE

A CIP catalogue record for this book is available
from the British Library

ISBN 0 7475 0830 5

10 9 8 7 6 5 4 3 2 1

Typeset by Hewer Text Composition Services, Edinburgh
Printed in Great Britain by Clays Ltd, St Ives plc

FOREWORD

There is no such newspaper as the *Glasgow Clarion*. That and everything else in this book is the product of my imagination.

I'd like to thank my friend Morag Malloy for her encouragement, and for being impressed by what she read rather than by what sycophants told her. Thanks are also in order to Bill Allsopp, Sergio Casci and Bill Kydd, and to Jim Murray for the best cup of tea in Scotland.

Thanks also to Jenny and Paul.

And to all the people who've come along to the readings.

And to Lucy, for lots of reasons.

The rest of you can kiss my arse.

Barry Graham

For Morag Malloy

Beware of what you want. You might get it.

> a girl who used to live next door to me.
> She said it was a Chinese proverb.

PROLOGUE

Stevie was hurt. He was hurt, and the roughness of the ropes at his back told him that he was also in trouble. A bomb went off inside his head and the floor came up to meet him, slamming into him with concussive force.

He was lying on his face.

So, he had to turn over. That was it. Yes. Turn over and then get up. Yes. Turn over. Turn over.

Turn over.

Screwing his eyes tightly shut, Stevie rolled onto his back. The noise of the crowd came to him as a distant roar, like the sound of water rushing through a tap. A thin, liquid vomit seared the back of his throat. He swallowed it down, pulled himself to his feet and opened his eyes. Four referees stood in front of him, and they all had the same face. All four spoke to him in the same voice, but he couldn't understand the Scots accent.

'Ramirez! Are you all right?' the quartet repeated, and this time Stevie understood. He nodded, even though he didn't feel all right at all.

The four referees became one. 'Box on,' he ordered, and this other Scotsman, this Ricky Mallon, came looking for the finish, bobbing, weaving, boring in. With all the force he could muster, Stevie slammed a right hand into Mallon's snarling face. Hurt and surprised, Mallon gave ground. At that moment the bell rang, ending the first round.

On shaking legs, Stevie walked to his corner and slumped on his stool. His trainer, Juan, removed his gumshield. Juan looked like a corpse. 'Jesus, Stevie. Jesus! Are you okay? Do you know where you are?'

'Yeah,' croaked Stevie. He had a heavy nosebleed and it was hard to speak. 'I'm in Scotland, getting the shit kicked out of me.'

Juan pinched Stevie's nostrils in an attempt to stop the bleeding. 'Do you want me to stop it?'

Stevie closed his eyes. 'If you do, I'll never speak to you again.'

Juan let go of Stevie's nose. The bleeding hadn't eased at all. Juan gave him a mouthful of water from a grimy bottle. 'You got to keep away from him,' he said. 'Got to box him. He can't box. Stick him. He's got no answer to a jab. Got to stick him. Stick him.' He wiped Stevie down with a sponge. The ten-second buzzer sounded. Juan patted his man's knee. His face was close to Stevie's, and his skin looked grey. His dark eyes seemed huge. 'Stick him,' he hissed. '*Stick him!*' He put the gumshield back in Stevie's mouth.

'Seconds out, round two.'

As the bell rang, the spectators began an eerie chant that echoed hollowly around the open-air stadium. The short, squat Mallon came after Stevie with maniacal ferocity. Stevie jabbed and moved out of distance. He tried to follow Juan's instructions, but his legs were full of pins and needles and he couldn't breathe. Mallon steamed after him, winging murderous blows with insane abandon. He cut off the ring and forced Stevie to the ropes, leaving him no option but to stand square-on and try to fight his way clear. He couldn't run away from Mallon for another ten rounds. Anything he did, he'd have to do now.

Stevie let go an overhand right that seemed to shake Mallon. The Scotsman didn't back off, but speared a left hook into Stevie's liver. Stevie dug in and fought back, and they traded punches in a frenzy. Blood was frothing down Stevie's throat from his nose and he tasted vomit. He wasn't sure whether he was still throwing punches. He couldn't see anything. He wondered if he was going to die.

Then everything became clear. He couldn't hear much, but he could see Mallon, hands down, chin exposed. Stevie tried to go after him, to bang in the left hook that would end it, but he found he was sitting on his stool and his seconds were holding him there and Juan knelt in front of him and said, 'Stop it, Stevie! It's over. *You were counted out!*' And he knew then.

Juan cleaned him up with the sponge. He could hear the spectators applauding their man, their man who'd just earned the right to fight Cetera, the world champion. Stevie already knew who'd win.

Some of Mallon's friends and some reporters had invaded the ring and crowded around his corner, eager to congratulate or interview him. No one came to Stevie's corner except for Billy Piers, a journalist who was once a very good fighter himself. He was a close friend of Mallon's, and Stevie was surprised to see him come over to *his* corner. The loser's corner is never a popular place.

Piers was a gaunt, bespectacled, gloomy-looking man in his mid-twenties. He reminded Stevie of Shaggy from *Scooby-doo*. He put a hand on Stevie's shoulder and squeezed. 'Well done. You fought a good fight. Made him work for it.'

'Thanks, man,' Stevie said, meaning it.

'Take it easy.' Piers went back to Mallon's corner.

Stevie's seconds helped him from the ring. He'd put on his robe, but he hadn't fastened the sash and it flapped open at the front. His mouth and throat were still clogged with blood and it hurt to swallow.

Stevie felt relieved.

ONE

It wasn't too squalid. The previous tenant'd had a cat and I could smell its piss. But as bedsits go it was better than many I'd lived in. The furniture was shabby and the bed sagged, but the room was big and there was a desk. There was a communal bog, kitchen and phone.

The place was on a busy corner, and on my first morning I woke to hear the big windows vibrating with the noise of the traffic. It wasn't the noise that woke me, though. That kind of noise hasn't been invented.

I got up, dressed and went downstairs to a newsagent. I flipped through some papers to see which had the most about Ricky. The *Glasgow Herald* had half a page and a photo, so I bought one and went back upstairs to read it.

In my room, I used my electric kettle to make some tea. I wasn't about to use the kitchen yet, one glance at it – and the bog – having told me that the other tenants must be among the filthiest bastards in Edinburgh. I'd soon sort that out.

I drank my tea and read the article. While I was reading it, the phone rang. I went out to the hall to answer it, knowing it'd probably be Ricky.

It was. 'Hi. Can I speak to Billy Piers?'

'You are,' I said.

'How're you feeling? Settling in?'

'I'm all right. I was just reading about you in the *Herald*.'

'I haven't seen a paper yet. What's it say?'

'Just that you're training in Edinburgh, and you're confident.'

'D'they say anything about him?'

'Not much. He's confident too. There's a lot of it about.'

He laughed. 'Are you coming to the gym today?'

'Uh-huh. What time're you starting at?'

'About two. D'you know where it is?'

'No, but I'll find it,' I said. 'Who else'll be there?'

'Just Norrie. Chris Moyer's coming through, but not till Monday.'

'I can probably manage a round or two,' I said.

It was just after eleven when I hung up. I typed up the shorthand notes I'd made in the gyms in Glasgow the week before. Then I cut the article about Ricky out of the *Herald* and put it in my file. I'd brought so little stuff, I'd been able to unpack it all when I moved in the previous night.

Ricky Mallon was the British Lightweight Champion. In around four weeks' time he was fighting for the world title in Glasgow, where we both came from. The place was buzzing with big-fight frenzy, so Ricky's manager had taken him to Edinburgh, where boxing and watching paint dry share the same attraction for the public. It meant he could train in peace. In Glasgow, he couldn't go out without being asked if he was Ricky Mallon. In Edinburgh, if he'd stopped people in the street and told them who he was, the reply'd have been either 'So what?' or '*Who?*'

Since the magazine I'd worked for had folded a year before, I'd been earning a very precarious living as a freelance journalist. I'd probably have starved if my articles on boxing hadn't been in such demand by both local and national papers. I'd been a reasonable pro fighter myself a few years ago, and no writer understands the game as well as I do.

Ricky and I'd been friends since I'd interviewed him after his first pro fight. He was now twenty-three, just a couple of years younger than me, and our friendship had managed to survive two years and the odd time I'd had to criticise him in print.

For the past few months I'd been considering doing a book about the British boxing scene. It'd be a collection of my articles, with additional, retrospective, comments. A publisher in London had shown interest, but I'd shelved the idea. I knew I had to get out of Glasgow.

At first I'd resisted the idea of leaving. But one day I was going down Buchanan Street when I heard this Jesus freak shouting about hell. The place actually sounded pretty good to me.

Then Ricky phoned to say he was setting up training camp in Edinburgh, in case I wanted to visit. That's when I got the idea. When hell sounds pleasant, Edinburgh's no problem. I thought about it for ten minutes, then called Ricky back.

'Listen. I've just had an idea for a book. About what it's like being part of the camp in the run-up to a world title fight. I don't mean just dropping in as a journalist, I mean actually being part of the camp. Working out with you, the lot. Right up till the fight.'

Ricky was enthusiastic. 'Norrie'll be into it. It'll be good publicity for us. And you'll be company for me.' I told the publisher who'd wanted to publish a collection of my articles, and he tentatively said he'd like to see the book.

Which is what I was doing in Edinburgh, though not why I was there. Ricky'd moved there a week before me, but I'd had some work to do that'd kept me in Glasgow.

While I was typing, the phone rang. I didn't answer it in case it was Karen. Nobody else answered it either. It rang for about five minutes. I went on typing all the time.

It was just after one when I left for the gym. It was freezing. I shivered in spite of my overcoat and two jumpers. The wind kept sweeping sheets of rain under my big golf umbrella, and I had to stop and wipe it from my glasses every couple of minutes.

Edinburgh's bus service is as bad as you'll find anywhere, but I was lucky and got one fairly soon. It being a Saturday, the bus was packed and I had to stand. I didn't mind. There was a bunch of coffin-dodgers sitting near me, and I listened in on their conversation. It was like a convention of surgeons and undertakers. By the time we reached Tollcross I'd learned that Charlotte's hip replacement had been a success, Clare didn't like her new dentist (he was just a *boy*, and a cheeky boy at that), this winter wasn't going to do Cathy's husband's chest any good, and the undertaker had done such a *lovely* job on Margaret. She'd looked so *nice* in the coffin just before they'd burnt her . . .

It didn't take me long to find the gym. It was in a disused shop that Norrie'd rented for four weeks. Norrie and Ricky were living in the flat upstairs from it.

A shutter was pulled down over the shop window, but the door opened when I pushed it. I went inside and looked around. Norrie'd made a good job of converting the shop to a gym; it was a bare, no-nonsense fighter's workplace. It was spacious, and a full-size ring had been erected in the middle of the floor. Two punchbags, heavy and light, hung from beams in the ceiling. There was also a speedball, floor-to-ceiling punchball, exercise mat and a mirror for shadow-boxing. There was no other equipment or furniture. The walls were grimy and the floor hadn't been swept.

Ricky was in the ring, punching the pads on Norrie's hands. They didn't stop or look at me. 'Changing room's in the back shop,' Norrie called. I went through. There were four wooden chairs, a shower, a sink, an electric kettle, tea bags and fruit scones. I changed into my training gear – shorts, vest, tube socks and boxing boots – then wrapped my hands with crepe bandage. I took the bag with the rest of my gear and went through to the gym.

Ricky and Norrie were still working with the pads. I got out my leather rope and skipped as I watched them. They were practising combinations. Ricky's punches were wild and inaccurate, but when he connected properly the force of it would nearly pull Norrie's arm off. And, on the pads, he hit lightly by his standards.

Ricky was five foot two, and weighed one hundred and thirty-five pounds. He was so heavily muscled that he gave the impression of having no neck. In fact, for such a fit guy, he didn't have much shape at all. He was just a mass of muscle with a cropped, blond head on top.

In his fighting style he was more American than British. He traded on all-out aggression and was the best pressure fighter I ever saw. From the first bell he'd go forward, rolling, weaving, grunting, snorting, throwing hook after hook with unrelenting fury. He never stopped and he never seemed to tire. Crude as it was, his style had a cleverness that wasn't always apparent to spectators. He didn't get hit half as often as most people thought. His constant bob-and-weave, combined with the sheer ferocity of his attack, made him difficult to catch cleanly. His opponents were usually too busy just trying to keep him off.

Ricky was undefeated in twenty-nine pro fights. The big question mark hung over his ability to sustain his frenzied fighting pace over the world championship distance of twelve three-minute rounds. He'd never been past eight. His British title fight had been scheduled for twelve, but he'd made all the speculation about his staying power academic by laying out the champion in the fifth.

Stamina probably wouldn't have much to do with the world title fight. Like Ricky, Michael Cetera was a rough, hustling fighter whose assets were strength and punching power. I couldn't see it going past five.

Ricky and Norrie came out of the ring. Ricky began some exercises on the mat. I got into the ring and shadow-boxed lightly, moving around. I'm not a bad boxer. I could never beat a really top-class fighter, but I'd lose on points without getting hurt. I'm a natural spoiler, with a jab-and-grab style that's boring to watch, but gets you through a few fights with some brain cells left at the end. Nobody wants to fight a spoiler, even if they know they can win easily. A spoiler makes you look bad. He's all elbows and gloves, and if you find something to hit that's not an arm or a glove or the top of a head, he'll grab you and hold on till the ref breaks it up. In seventeen pro fights, I was stopped only once. In my last fight.

I shuffled around the ring, starting to sweat. I felt all right. I'd kept reasonably fit during the three years I'd been out of the ring, and I didn't feel too rusty.

Norrie called to me. 'Billy, are you up to giving Ricky a move around?'

'If he goes easy.'

'Don't worry,' Ricky said. He was sweating heavily. 'It's just to get me moving. Nothing messy.'

Norrie greased both our faces with Vaseline, so the punches would slide off with less impact. Ricky put on a headguard. I didn't bother. I don't like them. They make you careless, and they give no real protection. Ricky didn't like them either, but now it was different. There must be no chance of his being cut, and even the minimal protection of a headguard was worth having.

I searched in my bag and found my gumshield. I put it in my mouth, and Norrie helped me on with the fourteen-ounce sparring gloves. I climbed into the ring and picked a corner. Norrie and Ricky got in. Ricky went to the opposite corner. He didn't look at me.

Norrie was holding a stopwatch. He set it and said, 'Get going, boys. Fast and light.' Ricky came out of his corner like an express train.

I moved to the centre of the ring, then shuffled to the side as he came at me. He turned to come after me and I jabbed, catching him on the forehead. At the same time, he brought over a left hook. I took it on my shoulder, but the force of it made me stagger.

'Ease up, Ricky. Fast and light,' said Norrie. 'Keep jabbing,

Billy. You're doing well.' I landed a few more jabs during the rest of the round. I went with Ricky, keeping myself covered and taking his punches on my arms and shoulders. When you're in with someone that strong, he's going to push you around. There's nothing you can do about it, and you'll only exhaust yourself if you try. It's best to move, spoil, and get your own in whenever you can. So I did.

Norrie called time. Ricky'd been handling me gently for him, but my body ached. It was scary to imagine what it'd be like if he hit me in earnest.

'There was a nice bit of boxing going on there,' said Norrie. He looked at me. 'Another round?'

I nodded. 'Just one more.'

In the second round I was slower, easier to get to. However fit you think you are, you don't realise how much it takes to box even one round properly till you're in there. I became tired with alarming suddenness, and Ricky's punches got through. He took no liberties, though. His punching was fast, not hurtful. When I went to the ropes, he did wind me with a hook to the body. I fired back at him with both hands and landed solidly a couple of times.

Norrie called time. Ricky and I stood grinning at each other. I was standing in a pool of sweat. 'I forgot what a useful boy you used to be,' said Norrie as he undid the laces on my gloves. But we both knew that my weight advantage of half a stone wouldn't stop Ricky breaking me in two if he felt like it.

'I'm not bad. Rusty, though,' I said.

'You're fucking awkward,' said Ricky. 'You're one big pair of arms. It's like sparring with a fucking octopus.'

I laughed. 'Are you doing any more today?'

'No. I was going to run later on, but Norrie says no.'

Norrie nodded. 'I don't like a fighter to run every day. You get stale. You should have one day off. We'll run tomorrow.' When he said 'we', it wasn't the managerial 'we' ('We got a cut in the second round, but we survived it and we knocked him out in the ninth'); he meant it. At the age of sixty, he still ran with his fighters, though at an easier pace than he made them set.

'I'll come too,' I said.

Ricky and I washed at the sink in the changing room. When we'd dressed, Norrie made some tea and we had a fruit scone each.

'So how do you think he's shaping up?' Norrie asked me.

'Good. I'm hardly a demanding sparmate, but I'm harder to hit than Cetera. He'll be able to get him all right.'

'I know I will,' said Ricky. He'd put on jeans and an Aran sweater that was too big for him. 'That's not what it's going to be about. But he'll be looking to do the same as me. He'll be throwing some punches himself.'

I didn't like that. 'You'll be far too strong for him,' I said.

When we'd finished our tea, Ricky asked if I fancied a game of chess. He'd been a fanatic since his girlfriend'd taught him to play.

I looked at my watch. 'Nah. It's after four. I'm going to look up a mate of mine.'

'Okay. How about tomorrow?'

'Okay.'

'What time're you running at?' I asked.

He looked at Norrie, who said, 'About ten.'

'Where'll I meet you?'

'Here.'

Norrie saw me out. 'Did you notice?' he asked me as we reached the front door.

'His bottle? I could hardly miss it. It's not like him.'

'I don't think he's scared of Cetera. But he lives for this fight. I think he's just scared he'll make a cunt of it.'

I could understand that. I'd been with Ricky when he'd earned the world title chance by knocking out Stevie Ramirez at Glasgow's Ibrox Stadium. He'd seemed unmoved by his victory until the two of us were alone in his flat an hour or so later. Without warning, he'd started to cry.

'I'm getting it,' was all he could say by way of explanation. 'I'm fucking *getting* it.'

His intensity didn't surprise me. He'd been dreaming of a world title since he was fourteen. Most people want lots of things. When your life has just one focus, one grail, and you get a chance at it, the idea of failing must be chilling.

Shortly after we became friends, I broke out in gooseflesh at something Ricky said to me. I already knew we'd a lot in common; we'd both spent our teens in care, and we'd never done any other kind of work before becoming pro fighters. But Ricky told me of a time just after he'd turned pro.

'I was living on the South Side. Every day I'd run a couple of laps of Victoria Park. But sometimes I'd do a longer run, right out to Giffnock.

'I'd run at night. It was winter, fucking freezing. It was pitch dark. The houses out there're like fucking palaces, some of them. The windows were so bright. I wished I could just go in and sit with them, you know?'

I knew. Ricky didn't seem to notice, but I was shivering. Just after I'd turned pro, I used to run through the affluent Bearsden area. And I felt, exactly as he would describe it, what Ricky was to feel.

And I ran fast and trained hard and sometimes even fought as hard – but not often. If there were uncanny similarities between Ricky and me, there was one essential difference: I had the instinct of a survivor, while he was a natural killer. I fought to live, then quit. He fought to live, then lived to fight. The risks of boxing scared me; Ricky didn't care. I remarked once that owning the whole of Giffnock wouldn't be much good to a vegetable. Ricky said he wasn't bothered as long as he'd be a rich vegetable.

We only had one opponent in common, and he was one of the greatest lightweights of this century: Wilfredo Santana of Panama, who won and lost the world title three times. He'd just lost it for the second time when I agreed to meet him in a ten-rounder at the Albert Hall in London.

I'd only had a fortnight's notice, coming in as a late substitute for someone who'd decided he'd rather stay in one piece. I was ten-to-one underdog, and even my manager expected me to lose.

I did, of course. I knew I would. But, where the fight should have been all over in two rounds with me lying inside-out on the canvas, it went ten and nobody got hurt. Santana was a brilliant boxer, a savage brawler and devastating puncher, but that night he had nobody to box, brawl with or punch. I kept jabbing, ran like a thief, covered up and held on like a leech whenever he got near me. That's how it went for ten rounds. I survived. In the final round, with less than a minute to go, I made him stop short with a right to the jaw, about the only one I threw that night. The ref scored that round even, giving all the rest to Santana. I was so exhausted I had to lie on the rubbing table for half an hour afterwards.

Ricky and Santana met shortly after I'd retired from boxing. Santana'd just lost his third world title and was a bit over the hill, but I reckoned a fighter of his class going in with a novice like Ricky was a bad mismatch.

That's how it seemed in the first couple of rounds. Santana could hit Ricky at will, and he did. Ricky kept pressing forward, banging his gloves together and inviting him to 'Come on, come on!'

Santana obliged. He stayed calm under Ricky's demented attack, blocking and slipping and counterpunching with horrible accuracy. Ricky kept coming. Jabs, hooks and overhand rights landed squarely, but he kept lunging forward and slinging wild hooks, most of which missed completely.

By the fifth round, Santana had run out of bombs and was throwing stones. Ricky was as strong as ever, and his punches were getting through. At first they only glanced off as Santana wrestled and smothered, looking to weather the storm and come back into the fight. But Ricky pushed him off and hit him hard. I was watching from the press bench, and by the end of the fifth I knew what was going to happen. I wrote in my notebook, '*KO or stoppage in round six(?).*' Sure enough, in the next round the ref had to stop it. Santana was still on his feet, but doubled over, clutching his sides. From where I sat I could hear his groans.

TWO

It was a year since I'd last been to Alan's place, a year since I'd last seen Alan. I'd only visited him that one time, a few days after he'd moved to Edinburgh. Since then, no contact. He wasn't on the phone. He never came to Glasgow and I never went to Edinburgh. We never wrote to each other. We never exchanged Christmas cards. He was my best mate and I loved him.

It was almost five when I arrived at Alan's flat in Comiston Road, Morningside. I knew he'd be expecting me. I'd sent him a note the week before. It was typical of us: *'I'm coming to Edinburgh next week. I'll come and see you on Saturday. Billy.'*

It was so long since I'd been there, I couldn't remember which flat it was. Then I saw his name on a door. *A. McManus.* I rang the bell, and when he opened the door it was as if we'd last met the day before.

'Hi.' He grinned at me. 'Come in.' He was six foot seven and weighed seventeen stone. He wore jeans and a sweat shirt that were splashed with paint. There was some paint in his black hair.

We went into the living room. The only furniture was a three-piece suite and a gas fire. There were no carpets on the polished wooden floor and no curtains at the windows.

I sat down in an armchair and Alan sprawled on the couch.
'How've you been?' he asked.

'Crap.'

'How come?'

'I'll tell you later. I'll get a cup of tea out of you first.'

'Yeah, I'll put some on in a minute. What're you doing in Edinburgh?'

'I'm with Ricky Mallon. The boxer.'

'Never heard of him.'

He'd never heard of anybody who wasn't an artist. 'You're an ignorant bastard,' I said. 'If you haven't heard of Ricky, you haven't been reading my articles.'

'I haven't. Didn't notice you at my exhibition in June. Or any of the others.'

'Mm. Maybe because I wasn't there.' We smiled at each other.

'Ricky's fighting for the world title in a few weeks. I'm thinking of doing a book about him, so I'm training with him.'

'Have you been boxing with him?'

'I did a couple of rounds today. Just playing about.'

'You'll be in Edinburgh a while, then?'

'Yeah.'

'How's Karen doing? Still together?'

'Sort of. It's sort of because of her that I'm here. I needed a break.'

'Is that what you meant about things being crap?'

'Yeah.'

'Not getting along?'

'Her illness is playing up.'

'Fuck. What happened?'

'It's just getting worse,' I said.

'What's her doctor say? Does he know?'

I nodded. 'They tried giving her some more medication, but it didn't do much good. I know it's not her fault, but it can be fucking horrible to live with.'

'What's she actually been doing?'

I hesitated. 'Forget the tea. Let's go for a drink instead.'

'Okay.' He looked at his paint-splashed clothes. 'I'd better change.'

'Yeah. Can I see what you've been painting?'

'Uh-huh.' He took me through to the room he used as a studio. 'You won't like it.'

I knew that already. As far as art goes, I'm a card-carrying Philistine. Alan's work was selling well. To me, it was just sheets of canvas smeared with paint and bits of newspaper rolled up and stuck together with glue.

I used to like to wind him up at parties. 'This is Alan,' I'd tell people. 'He's an artist. I'll show you some of his stuff.' And I'd roll a sheet of newspaper and drop it on the floor, or smear tomato ketchup over a paper towel.

'This is just a rough. I've only started it,' he said, opening the door of the studio. The light was already on. It was very bright. The room was large and unfurnished except for one wooden chair. A couple of Alan's newspaper sculptures lay on the floor. The walls were covered with pieces of paper on which he'd scribbled thought fragments and descriptions of images, most of which he'd use in his paintings. (I'm not clever – I only know because he told me.)

On the wall near the window was a canvas with paint on it. 'That's my baby,' said Alan. 'My work-in-progress. You can think up some insults while I get changed.'

He went out. I had a look at the painting. It might have been a house or a castle. It also might have been a bath with somebody drowning in it. God or Alan only knew what it actually was. He was right. I didn't like it.

As I waited for him to come back, I read some of the notes stuck to the wall. Most of them were affected and self-indulgent, but there was one I liked. The sly ambiguity of it was lost on me at the time, but it was to haunt me for days afterwards.

Underneath a question mark, Alan had written two lines:

Is love just another word for hope
(never realised!)

It's on the wall above the desk I'm writing at now.

'Whereabouts're you living?' asked Alan. We were walking to his car. It was raining again.

'Newington. I've got a bedsit in Newington Road.' We ended up going over there. It'd save me the bother of getting back later, and Alan knew a pub there.

The drive took about ten minutes. The rain got heavier. 'Are you and Karen going to split?' Alan asked as he drove.

'I don't know. We might. I don't know what'd happen to her if we did.'

'I thought it was under control.'

'A year ago it was. She just took her medication and heard the occasional voice.'

'So what's happening now?'

'If I gave you the list, we'd be up all night. A couple of months ago, she broke a glass over her head. Said there was a baby inside her head and she had to kill it.'

'Fuck's sake.' He looked shocked. He'd been fond of Karen.

'That was only things warming up. I don't even want to talk about some of the things she's done since then.'

'What's her shrink say?'

'They've changed the diagnosis. It used to be schizophrenia. That means they don't know what the fuck's wrong with you, but they can give you some stuff to keep you from getting too crazy. But now they've decided she's got a personality disorder.'

'Which means?'

'It means they still don't know what's wrong with you, but they haven't any dope that treats it.'

'Fuck,' he said again. 'Is there any chance of them locking her up?'

'Not much, according to her shrink. She'd have to break the law or something. So far, she's been no threat to anybody but herself. Though,' I added as he stopped the car outside the pub, 'if I hadn't got away from there, I think I'd have ended up crazier than she is.'

It was the sort of pub Alan liked, furnished with wall-to-wall forty-five-year-old gin-and-tonic drinkers. A notice on the wall behind the bar read: *Please do not ask for credit, as a punch in the mouth often causes offence.*

'What d'you want?' asked Alan. 'Is it still Guinness?'

'Yeah.'

I went and found a table. Alan came over with Guinness for me and lager for himself. We talked idly for a while, though we both knew the conversation would come back to Karen. He asked how I'd financed the stay in Edinburgh, and I told him I planned to do some articles about Ricky for the *Glasgow Clarion* and other papers. If I couldn't sell them I'd be in the shit, though I knew that wasn't likely.

After a while I got hungry. I'd barely eaten during the day. I went up to the bar to ask if they served food. I had to wait a couple of minutes to be served. As I waited, the memory of Karen's most recent incident came back with disturbing clarity.

I'd gone to London to cover the Harkin-Abbott British heavyweight title fight for the *Glasgow Clarion*. The next morning I arrived back in Glasgow, gave my report to the paper and thought that was the end of it. But that night – or rather two o'clock the following morning – the phone rang in the West End flat I shared with Karen.

It takes more than a phone ringing next to the bed to wake Rip Van Billy. Karen answered it and shook me awake. 'It's for you.'

'Who is it?' I said groggily. 'If it's not work, tell them to fuck off.'

'It must be work. It's Perring.'

I took the phone. Ghengis Perring was the *Clarion*'s sports editor. He was also known as Attila the Journalist for his methods of running the sportsdesk.

'Piers.'

'Hi, Billy. Frank Perring here.'

'So I hear. What's up?'

'A story. Can you come down to the office? Right now?'

'What's the story?'

'Abbott killed himself tonight.'

'What – *Neil* Abbott?' Abbott was the winner of the fight I'd covered the night before. I was quite friendly with him.

'Uh-huh. The way he did it was fucking horrible, too,' said Perring. 'I'll tell you when I see you. You knew him, didn't you?'

'Yeah. Though he wasn't an intimate.'

'Can you come in and do a story?'

'Yeah. I'll be there in twenty minutes.'

I got out of bed and stretched. *Neil Abbott.* 'I'll have to go down to the *Clarion*,' I told Karen. 'One of the fighters I was watching last night killed himself.' She didn't answer, just lay on her back with her eyes open.

I put on jeans and a jumper and went through to the living room to get my contact book and concertina file. I put on my coat and went back to the bedroom.

'I'm not sure how long I'll be – ' I broke off. Karen was curled up on the bed, her face twisted as she cried soundlessly.

I looked at her, dumbstruck. 'What's up?'

'Nothing. Just go.' She went on crying.

'Karen, *what's wrong?*' I sat down on the bed and put my hand on her naked shoulder. She shrugged it off and cried even harder.

'Piss off,' she sobbed. 'Just go and meet whoever you're going to meet.' I tried to touch her hair and she slapped at my hand.

'Karen, you *know* who I'm going to meet. He's just been on the phone.'

'*Fucking go, then!*' she spat out with a venom that shook me so badly I just turned and went.

I drove to the Clydeside office of the *Glasgow Clarion* in the ancient mini that gave up on me for good a few weeks later. I was shocked, angry and frightened all at once. I could hardly believe what Karen'd said, let alone understand it.

From outside, the *Clarion* building looked more like an old warehouse than a major newspaper office. The guy at reception knew me, and I walked past him without showing my press card. I took the lift to the second floor, where the newsroom was.

It was a huge, open-plan office. The sportsdesk was at the halfway mark, next to the newsdesk. During the day eight people could be found sitting round it, but now there was only Ghengis Perring and another sportswriter called Dick Kravitz, who didn't like me.

'You look tired,' said Perring.

'Being got out of bed does that to me. What happened?'

'He poked both of his eyes out with a pair of scissors. Died before they could get him to hospital.'

'Christ.'

'Any idea why he might've done it?'

'None at all. Christ,' I said. 'The guy'd just won the British title. He was walking on air.'

'Well, he came back down to earth pretty fucking quick,' Perring said.

'What d'you want me to do?'

'Right now, can you put together a personal piece? Impressions of the fight, the man himself and so on?' I nodded. 'We can put that in tomorrow's issue with the news of the death. First thing in the morning, get on to everybody that knew him and see what they can tell you.'

'I'll probably have to go back to London, then,' I said.

'Go, then.'

'Okay. I'll get a flight tomorrow. Today, rather.'

I opened my concertina file at A and found the very few articles and notes I had on Abbott. Combined with Perring's news report from London, it still didn't add up to a lot of information, but it was as much as I needed for the subjective piece I was about to write.

I had it written by three-thirty. I've never had a problem writing good copy quickly. I've never missed a deadline, and it's been a long time since an editor asked me to rewrite a story.

Perring read it and approved. He sent it to be typeset, and we just sat around for a couple of hours, talking and drinking tea. He asked about the progress of my proposed book, *Billy Piers on Boxing*. I said I was working on it. If I'd said I'd abandoned it, he'd have asked why.

At seven a.m. I decided it was late enough to start phoning people. I called Neil Abbott's wife and his manager, Owen Dillon. Neither'd been asleep when I rang. Neither had any idea why Abbott had killed himself. They agreed that he'd been elated after the fight. I said I'd be in London later that day, and they both agreed to be interviewed.

At seven thirty-five, the phone rang. I answered it mainly to annoy Dick Kravitz, who resented freelancers (ie peasants) behaving like staff. 'Sportsdesk.'

'Can I speak to Mr Piers, please?' asked a male voice. That was odd; there was no reason for anyone to think I'd be at the *Clarion*.

'You already are. Who's this?'

'I'm Sergeant Jaffrey, from Pitt Street Police Station.'

Then I knew. 'Uh-huh?'

'We've just had a visit from a Miss Northey. She's made some strange claims.'

'Such as?'

'She says that you intend to rape her. And there's a conspiracy to murder her, led by a man named Perring.'

'Jesus.' I wasn't in shape for this. I explained that Karen

Northey was a diagnosed schizophrenic and sometimes suffered from delusions. I added that, having lived with her for some time, I so far hadn't found it necessary to rape her, and didn't expect to. Mr Perring, I said, was sports editor of the *Glasgow Clarion*, and, while he undoubtedly had his faults, as far as I knew a tendency to kill people wasn't among them.

'I see. I thought it'd be something like that. She seemed a bit odd.'

'She is. Is she still there?'

'No. She left after she'd made her complaint.'

'Oh.' I started to worry.

'Thanks, Mr Piers. Sorry to have bothered you.'

'No bother.' I rang my flat. There was no answer.

The newsroom was getting busier as the day shift arrived. I looked around for Perring. 'I might have to pass by going to London.'

'*What?*' His face became livid in seconds.

'I said *might*. I've got a problem.'

'What problem? What problem?'

'Not with the article. It's personal, and it might be serious.'

'"Might be"? It'd better be fucking serious. What're you playing at?'

I was being as unprofessional as it's possible to be. 'I'm sorry. I'll still try to make London. I've got to find somebody. If I find her quickly I'll still make it.'

'"Her"? What the fuck is this, girlfriend trouble? You're letting a story go down the toilet because of trouble with your fucking girlfriend!'

'Frank, if I don't make it you can send Kravitz.'

If he'd been angry before, now he became furious. 'Oh, come *on*. You know, and I know, that Dick's not in your league. As far as boxing's concerned, nobody is. Dick would go to London and come back with less of a story than you'd get from a couple of phone calls.'

'I'm sorry,' I said again. I picked up my file and contact

book and turned to go. 'I'll phone and let you know by eleven.'

I was almost out of the newsroom when Perring caught up with me.

'I'll tell you one thing,' he said in a low voice. 'If you let this story go, don't even bother to say hello when you see me in the street.'

There was nothing I could say. He was right.

I drove to my flat to see if Karen'd come back. She hadn't. I drank a mug of tea and wondered what to do. *Oh, Kerry, why aren't you here? I need you.* Outside it began to rain heavily. I knew Karen couldn't have gone to visit any of her friends. They'd all be at work. Karen'd been unemployed since the start of her illness.

So where would she be? I knew she liked to wander around the shops and cafés in the Byres Road area. She was as likely to be there as anywhere.

That's where she was. After leaving the police station, she'd briefly gone back to the flat. She heard a voice telling her to look down at her feet. She looked, and her feet seemed to be receding, disappearing into her ankles. The voice told her to go to the bathroom and make her nose bleed. She stood in front of the bathroom mirror and slapped herself till she bled. The voice then told her she was the devil, and she must go to Byres Road. She went. Once there, other voices began telling her what to do. One would tell her to get on a bus. Once on it, another voice would scream at her to get off. This went on, she told me, for a long time. She always got off the buses before they left Byres Road.

It was in Byres Road I found her, soaked through, confused and terrified. I got her into my car and she clung to me, shivering violently and saying she was sorry and I stupidly told her not to worry and she asked would I leave her and I said of course not and I almost believed myself.

I took her home, peeled the wet clothes off her and got

her into a warm bath. It was five-past eleven. I phoned her friend Morag at the office where she worked.

'Hello, Morag? It's Billy Piers. Listen, could you possibly take the afternoon off work? Karen's had a bit of an upset. Uh-huh. Uh-huh. Pretty bad, yeah. I can't leave her alone, but I've got something I have to do. Yeah, work. I know, but I've got to. They like me to pay the mortgage once in a while. Great. I really appreciate it, Morag. How long'll you be? Great. Thanks, Morag.' I hung up.

I went through to the bathroom. Karen was huddled in the bath, still shivering slightly. 'You're going away,' she mumbled.

I bent down and kissed her on the cheek. 'Don't talk rubbish. I've got to go to London, but I'll be back late tonight.'

She looked at me like a child. 'Promise?'

'Promise,' I said. I kissed her again, very softly. Some of her black curls had fallen over her eyes. I pushed them back and grinned at her. 'I promise, you idiot! I'm not going to leave you.'

Suddenly, she smiled widely at me. 'I love you,' she said.

'You've got good taste. I love you. I phoned Morag. She's coming to stay with you till I get back.'

'Good. But come back as quick as you can.'

I phoned Perring and told him to get me a flight to London. Huffily, he said he would. He rang back a couple of minutes later to tell me my flight was at one.

I was back in Glasgow at two in the morning, with my story already written. It would appear in the *Clarion* under the heading *Death of a Heavyweight*, and eventually get me in the running for a Journalist of the Year award. Perring said it was the best sports article the paper had ever published.

When I arrived in Glasgow I went to the *Clarion* office, keyed the story into the direct input system, then headed home. I'd barely slept at all in the past forty-eight hours, and I was so tired it was almost like being drunk. But as I neared my flat I felt a sensation of dread at the thought of getting into bed next to Karen, and I hated myself for it. I needed to speak to Kerry, and there wasn't much chance of that.

The memory'd come back so vividly that when the barman asked me what I wanted, it was as if he, and not the image of Glasgow, was unreal. It took a couple of seconds to make sense of the noises coming out of his mouth.

I asked if the bar served food, and he said they did toasties. They were into cheese; you could have cheese and bacon, cheese and onion, cheese and tomato or cheese. I asked for four cheese and tomato, and he said he'd bring them over.

I sat down next to Alan. 'You should've said you were hungry,' he told me. 'You could've had something at my place.'

'I wasn't hungry then.'

Silence for a moment, then he said, 'D'you still love Karen?'

He'd never asked me anything like it before. 'Why?'

'You know why.'

'I don't. Why?'

'You're talking as if Karen being mental was something new. When I lived in Glasgow, she was practically swinging from the rafters before she got her medication.'

'I know. I was there. So what?'

'You didn't think about leaving her then.'

I didn't answer.

'I'm not trying to give you a hard time. I'm just wondering. I mean, I'm not saying you shouldn't leave her. It's just that at one time you didn't want to. I mean, is she any crazier now?'

'No. Not really,' I said. 'Her worst now's about the same as her worst back then.'

'So you don't feel the same about her?'

'No.'

'If I'm prying, tell me to mind my own business.'

'No, I don't mind.'

'Is there somebody else?' he asked.

The barman brought over a plate with four greasy cheese and tomato toasties. The bread was white and tasteless, but I was hungry enough to kill a tramp and put him between two rancid mattresses.

'You're half right,' I told Alan. 'There is somebody else, sort of. I'm not fucking her or anything. Doesn't look like I'm going to, either.'

'Anybody I know?'

'No. Her name's Kerry. I met her after you moved through here. She moved in next door.'

'Mm. Does Karen suspect anything?'

'No. There's nothing to suspect. I told you, nothing's happened.'

'I take it this girl's not so keen on you?'

I couldn't help laughing. 'That's about right. And I haven't seen her in months. She's been working down south.'

'If she felt the same about you, would you leave Karen?'

'Probably.'

As we were walking the short distance from the pub to my flat, Alan asked, 'Have you ever been unfaithful to Karen?'

Whatever my answer was, I knew it wouldn't shock him. Even when Alan's going steady, he fucks around as if his primary goal in life is to catch AIDS.

'Never,' I said. 'I've thought of it plenty of times, but I wouldn't do it.'

'Not even with this Kerry? If you were able to?'

'Maybe. But I'd tell Karen. I wouldn't carry on seeing Karen and just fuck Kerry on the side. But I told you. It's not going to happen.'

When we arrived at my bedsit, I found that somebody'd tidied the kitchen. I made some toast and we took it through to my room. I boiled the electric kettle to make some tea.

'Taken up baseball?' Alan was looking at the baseball bat propped next to the door.

'No. It's for splitting heads.' I poured the tea.

'Yeah, I thought that. Expecting bother?'

'Nah. Force of habit. I'd some bother in Glasgow a while ago. I got into the habit of keeping the bat by the door. It's a handy household implement.'

He laughed. 'Was it the bother about that show you ran?' I nodded. 'I read something about it,' he said.

'Probably. It made most of the Scottish papers.'

We were talking about a boxing show I'd co-promoted with Norrie Wilson nearly a year before. Norrie'd wanted to run a show in Glasgow. It'd let Scottish boxing fans have a look at Ricky, who'd been fighting mostly in England. At the time, I was deputy editor of *The Voice* magazine, and had some money saved. I offered to split the costs of the promotion, and the profits, with Norrie. He accepted and we went ahead.

The show was held in the Plaza Ballroom on Glasgow's South Side. It attracted a lot of local interest, but there were problems. Glasgow's principal boxing promoter and manager at the time was Kevin Wood, a man I hated, and who'd hated me, since I'd first appeared on the boxing scene. Wood wasn't a boxing man. He was a dirty little thug who'd got hold of licences to manage and promote. He'd bought his way into boxing. He was so low he'd have had to ascend to get into hell.

Trouble was, Wood didn't like it when somebody else tried to run a show in 'his' city, and he owned just about every decent pro fighter in Scotland. Norrie phoned him and asked if he'd give us some fighters to make up half of the bill. 'I wouldn't give you the pickings of my nose if you were starving,' Wood replied and hung up.

A contact of mine in Belfast saved us from having to call off the promotion. He sent over a squad of Irish fighters to help make up the bill. They were good names, and by the day of the show we'd sold tickets for more than half of the seats, and expected the rest to be filled by those who paid at the door.

But, that morning, I was wakened by a phone call from Norrie. 'What the fuck's this in the *Clarion*?' he demanded.

'What?'

'Go and get a paper. You'll understand then.' I did. And I understood only too well.

On the sports page there was a news item, announcing that I'd phoned to say that the show'd had to be called off at the last moment, and that ticket-holders were to write to me or Norrie to get their money back.

I phoned the *Clarion* and asked to speak to Perring. They said he was on holiday, and the hoax call had been taken by Dick Kravitz. Ten minutes later, Perring phoned me from home. 'What's this about a call-off?'

'Fucking sabotage's what it is,' I told him. 'Somebody claiming to be me phoned and told Kravitz the show was off, and he went and published it without checking.'

'Christ.' Perring was aghast. 'I'll fillet the little bastard before I sack him.'

'Nah, don't blame him. He can't help being a retard.'

'D'you think it was Kevin Wood?'

'I fucking know it was,' I said.

There wasn't much to be done. Norrie and I went through our list of people who'd bought tickets, phoned them and told them the show was still on. Then we put up a notice outside the door of the Plaza saying: '*Tonight's boxing show has NOT been cancelled*.' But that was all we could do.

Most of the ticket-holders showed up, and we sold about a dozen tickets on the door, but that still left about a third of the seats empty. The show was good. Ricky's fight was over in the first round, but there were some exciting battles among the other bouts. The best show that nobody saw, Norrie called it.

Financially, we survived. The show ran at a loss, but the *Clarion* at least compensated us for our costs. At my request, Perring didn't sack Dick Kravitz, but he had him writing obituaries and making tea for a long time.

About a fortnight later, I was at a show in the Albany Hotel. I was watching the first fight of the evening when somebody tapped me on the shoulder. It was Kevin Wood.

'So you've been saying I sabotaged your show?' he said coldly. He was the fattest, ugliest, most wart-ridden fuckpig I ever saw. His appearance was the best thing about him.

'That's right. Sue me for slander.' I looked away.

'You're asking to get your legs broken, Piers.'

I turned on him. 'Come out to the car park and break them, you fat cunt.' He just looked at me. 'Come on! I'll put your teeth so far down your throat you'll have to stick your toothbrush up your fat arse. Come on.'

He couldn't believe what he was hearing. You didn't speak this way to Mr Wood, spiritual grandson of Al Capone. I knew he probably had a couple of his heavies near at hand, but they wouldn't dare touch me in the hall. And, if he accepted my invitation to the car park, his boys wouldn't give it to me before at least one other was ready for a wheelchair.

Wood knew that too, and he knew it might be him. That's probably why he said, 'You prick,' and walked out of the hall.

Of course, that wasn't the end of it. I started getting threatening phone calls. They made me a little uneasy and scared Karen shitless, so I bought the baseball bat.

I needed it twice. The first time was when I opened my door to find two of Mr Wood's employees waiting for me. They said they'd like a word with me, and I told them to fuck off. Then, obviously not being of a conversational bent, one of them pulled a blade. The baseball bat was in the hall just next to the front door, and I used it to break both his legs and one of his arms. The other would've got something similar if he'd run a bit slower than he did.

Of course, when the pigs interviewed my victim in hospital, he wouldn't say who'd sent him. Then I got a phone call from Wood, saying he wanted to see me. He said he'd be at my flat in about half an hour. I said that would be very nice and hung up.

When his car pulled up outside my flat, I took the bat and went downstairs. I was surprised to see that Wood was on his own in the car.

He wound down a window and forced a smile. 'Hello, Billy. Get in the motor. This can't go on, can it? We'll have to talk.'

I didn't answer. I just set about trashing his Merc. I used the bat to knock in the windshield first. Wood, who was starting to say something else, screamed with fright. I knocked in the side and rear windows. I was seeing to the roof as a terrified Wood started the engine. I got in a few more good whacks before he drove away.

The threatening phone calls carried on. Wood threatened to set fire to my flat, and I'd no reason to think he was kidding. Mercifully, he died a few weeks later, when a lorry ran into his Merc. Norrie and I drank to his death.

'Fuck's sake.' Alan shook his head when I'd told him the story. 'What've I been missing!'

I grinned. 'I know. Life hasn't been quiet. Usually, I don't mind. But now I just want to lie low and write my book.'

'Are you going to see Karen while you're here?'

'Not if I can help it. If she asks to come through and visit, I'll say I'm too busy. She might come anyway, though. You know what she's like.'

'When'll you see the other one?'

'Kerry. Another few weeks. I don't know exactly. She's going to ring and let me know.'

'Where is she now?'

'Shropshire. She's been working down there.'

'Yeah, you said. What's she do?' he asked.

'She's an optician.'

A pause, then he said, 'Just how keen are you?'

'I think I love her. In fact, I'm sure I do.'

'So, if she feels the same, you'll leave Karen?'

'I told you, she doesn't feel the same. It's a question of race.'

'How come?'

'She only goes out with members of the human race.'

He didn't smile. 'What if she does feel the same?'

'I don't know. I know I'd want to leave Karen for her. Maybe I want to leave her anyway, or I wouldn't be here. But it'd finish her if I left. I don't know if I could put her through it. I mean, you know what happened to – '

'I know. It's a cunt of a thing to happen to any kid. But you didn't have the perfect childhood yourself.'

'Compared with hers, mine was right out of *The Waltons*.'

'I wouldn't go that far. And you're not responsible for what happened to her.'

'I know. But still.'

'I really like her,' said Alan. 'But if you don't want her, you're not doing her any favours by hanging around.'

'I know that. I'll figure something out.'

'You could do a lot worse than stay in Edinburgh,' he said. 'There're worse places.'

'Yeah. It's only the Scottish AIDS capital.'

'So? Just make sure you wear a condom when you share needles.'

I laughed. 'We'll see what happens.' *What about you, Kerry? You could do a lot worse too. There're worse places than here. There're worse people than me. And you should know.*

Alan stayed until four in the morning and I told him much more. There was a blank year in our friendship, and we were still as close as two men can be without bottoms becoming involved.

THREE

I arrived at the gym at ten on the Sunday morning. Ricky and Norrie, already in their tracksuits, were sitting on the ring apron when I went in.

'There's some terrible news,' said Norrie.

'The fight's not off?'

'Worse than that,' Ricky deadpanned, and I knew it could only be one thing.

'Not Murdo.' I closed my eyes. 'Please God, not Murdo.'

'He's tracked us down,' said Norrie. 'He shoved his new poem under the door about an hour ago.'

'It's his best ever,' Ricky added. 'Show it to him, Norrie. It's a classic.' Norrie handed me a typed sheet.

Murdo Donald was arguably the worst poet in human history. He was forty-five, going on for twelve. He wrote poems (for want of a better word) that made McGonigall seem like T.S. Eliot. He was a boxing fan and for nearly a year had been Ricky's groupie. Wherever Ricky trained, Murdo would find him and bombard him with poem after excruciating – and, naturally, unpublished – poem.

I read this latest masterpiece with awe. 'Fuck's sake.'

In the interests of literature, I feel compelled to print it here.

GLADIATOR OF THE SLUMS
by
Murdo Donald

Ricky Mallon was a boxer man,
Who fought from Glasgow to Taiwan.
Fists of steel and built like a door,
He was never known to touch the floor.

Amongst men a boxer,
Amongst boxers a man,
'Twixt fiddle and bow
One does what one can.

For he was a refugee from the slums,
Not from fear, from boredom.
He did not become neurotic,
Nor hide behind the use of narcotics.

For he was made of sterner stuff,
And, deciding that he'd had enough,
Did that which he knew was rightful,
And won the British lightweight title.

– But! He had not yet reached the heights,
Upon which he had set his sights.
Boxing is a gladiatorial biz,
And the world title shall soon be his.

I'm not kidding.
'D'you think he'll come and see you?' I asked Ricky.
'When does he not? Come on, get changed. I want to get
going before he shows up.'
I changed into a tracksuit and training shoes, and we drove
to Princes Street Gardens. It was a cold day and the park was
empty. Ricky and I set off at a smart pace as Norrie trotted
along a few yards behind us.
'Look.' Ricky pointed. Just ahead of us, at the edge of
the path we were running along, was a grey squirrel. It was

nibbling at something between its front paws, and took no notice of us as we ran past.

'Yeah. There's a lot of them in this park,' I said, and we were silent again.

As Ricky and I maintained our pace, Norrie's grew slower and slower. After about fifteen minutes he was hardly more than walking, and we'd passed him twice.

'Have you heard from Liz since you got here?' I asked. Ricky's girlfriend was a friend of Karen's.

'Uh-huh. I phoned her last night, and she phoned me this morning.'

'How's she doing?' I knew Liz doted on him. She'd have used his shit for toothpaste.

'Pissed off she can't see me.'

I could believe it. Karen'd told me Liz's feelings about not being allowed near Ricky till after the fight. But he was right not to see her. A fighter who has sex in training is as well not training at all. And, even if they saw each other without fucking, any distraction is bad.

'You're best that way,' I told him. 'You'll need your mind on the job. Especially for this one.'

'That's what I told her.'

He'd slackened the pace to let me get breath enough to speak. From somewhere behind us, Norrie shouted to pick it up. We did.

'Pity about your eyesight,' Ricky said. 'Since you're getting so fit, we could've got you an eight-rounder.'

I grunted. I didn't have the breath to say anything. I wondered if Ricky really thought I'd ever consider fighting again. He was right about my eyesight; I wouldn't stand a chance of passing a boxing medical. But Ricky knew my short-sightedness had nothing to do with my quitting boxing. The eye trouble'd come long afterwards.

My last fight: Victor Gezuli was a lightweight executioner who was avoided like syphillis on the boxing scene. Since escaping to London from South Africa two years before, he'd proven himself willing – and very able – to fight anyone, anywhere, with no more notice than he needed to pack his bag and travel to the venue in time for the fight. He'd lost one or two, but on close points decisions against top fighters, who were usually heavier than him to boot. He called himself the Man of Steel, and boasted that nobody could put him down. Most people – especially those he fought – were inclined to believe him.

I was asked to fight him at a week's notice. I accepted because, in spite of his reputation, I reckoned his face-first style would be no problem for me.

The fight was at the Kelvin Hall, Glasgow. As soon as I arrived there, I'd a bad feeling. The familiar smell of impending pain, the smell of a boxing show, seemed stronger than usual. It's a delightful little perfume of beer, old leather, Vaseline and festering armpits.

My fight was top of the bill. I felt a cold insect crawl over my testicles as the referee called Gezuli and me to ring centre for the final instructions. Gezuli wasn't heavily muscled, but lithe and capable-looking. We didn't look at each other's faces.

'. . . Shake hands now, go back to your corners and come out fighting at the bell,' said the ref. I touched gloves with Gezuli and went to my corner. My manager, Rab Edkin, put my gumshield into my mouth.

'Work hard, now,' he told me. 'Don't let him rest. And don't get involved in a brawl. Keep jabbing and moving. Don't let him settle down, be the boss from the start. But be careful, right?'

'Right.'

'Seconds out, round one.'

The bell rang. I darted out to the middle of the ring, chin tucked down, hands held high. Gezuli came out in a frenzy, scorning defence, slinging wild left hooks in an attempt to end the fight there and then. I moved away, flicking out a few jabs. They landed squarely, but lightly. I got my distance and jabbed more solidly. Gezuli hadn't landed a punch yet, and I couldn't seem to miss him. Taking a chance, I moved to meet him, slipped one of his big hooks and crossed over a right hand. It caught him on the side of the jaw and he fell heavily on his side.

'Up! Up! *Up!*' I heard Gezuli's trainer scream. He needn't have worried; staying down never entered his man's head. He rose at the count of eight and fought back like a wounded lion. I abandoned my usual cautious boxing as I went to finish him, and we battered each other with furious punches to head and body. I sent his gumshield flying from his mouth, and we were both bleeding heavily from our noses when the bell rang.

'Fucking *box him*, you stupid cunt!' snarled Rab as I dropped on to my stool. 'You had him there and you let him off the hook. Now get back in there and sort the fucker. Get him again, then stand back, keep the head – *and finish him off!*'

'Seconds out, round two.'

Gezuli was on top of me as soon as the bell rang and, far from being able to do as Rab said, I found myself fighting for my life. I couldn't seem to get my boxing together, and he staggered me so badly I almost went down. I raged back and we tore into each other. We didn't hear the bell, and the ref had to separate us and shove us back to our corners.

Rab sponged my face as Jim, the assistant second, held out the waistband of my shorts to ease the agony of my battered midriff. Rab offered me the water bottle but I shook my head.

'Now, listen. You're hurt and he's hurt. How bad d'you want to win this fight?'

'Bad,' I rasped.

'Right.' Rab's face was grim. 'Stay the fuck away from him, right? Stay away and *box him*. He's fucking dangerous with those big hooks.'

'You're telling me.' My head felt muddy. 'Don't worry, I'll get him.'

He put in my gumshield. 'Tighten your guard. Keep him

out. And fucking batter him every time he tries to get near you. Go on.'

I stood up and took a deep breath. Gezuli was still on his stool, and across the twenty feet between us I heard every word of his second's instructions. 'Get in there, forget defence, batter the big lanky bastard right round the ring – *and then knock him right out of it!*'

'Seconds out, round three.'

Gezuli's face looked sick and puffy, his eyes bright with venom. As he came after me I set myself, got my distance and jabbed him four times. He eased his attack, not liking it, and started to box. That suited me. I jabbed him once more, then hurt him with a right to the side of the head. He swayed. I went forward, and walked straight into a crushing right. I dropped to my knees.

I shuddered with fury as the ref counted over me. I wasn't going to let it end like this. If I could survive another two rounds, I was sure I could still outbox him and get the decision. I struggled to my feet as the count reached eight. The ref looked at me uncertainly, then ordered, 'Box on.'

Gezuli was all fighter. Weary and hurt though he was, he saw his chance and wasn't about to let it pass by. He rushed me right away, arms flailing like some demented octopus. A cruel, perfectly timed left hook dumped me on the seat of my shorts. I managed to drag myself up, but my legs folded under me and I sprawled on the canvas. There was a brief blackout, then the ref was helping me to the corner. Rab and Jim helped me sit down shakily on my stool. Wordlessly, Rab ruffled my hair. Jim's face was drained of colour. That, and the hush that'd fallen over the crowd, told me that I really had been beaten badly.

Gezuli came over and hugged me. 'You okay?'

'Yeah. I think you just knocked me sensible.'

After a while, Norrie stopped running and went to sit in the car. Ricky and I kept running, but slowed our pace considerably. In the distance we could see Arthur's Seat, the famous hill just outside the city. In the cold, against the grey sky, it was as beautiful as anything I'd seen.

'We should take a hike up there sometime,' I said.

'Yeah. When?'

'Soon as you like.'

'What about Tuesday, after training?' he said.

'Yeah. Fine.'

Norrie called us to the car. 'How're you feeling?' he asked Ricky as we got in.

'Good. I'm hardly breathing heavy.'

As he started the car, Norrie looked at me and said, 'You're looking pretty good as well.'

'I feel okay. Better than I expected to. The sparring'll get me really fit.'

'How much sparring d'you want to do?' he asked.

'A fair bit, but no wars. I'll move around with Ricky, and have a go with the other guys too, if they want. Who else is coming?'

'Chris Moyer's coming tomorrow. Steve Tambourini's coming tomorrow or Tuesday. He's phoning us tonight to let me know.'

That was bad news; Tambourini was a born liberty taker in sparring. He was capable of fouls most referees hadn't even heard of, and was as willing to commit them in sparring as he was in a fight.

'Is that a good idea?' I said. 'I've sparred with Tambourini. He's a good mover, but he's dangerous. If you get on top, he's liable to try to hurt you. I mean, injure you. In one round with him, I got thumbed in the eye, half strangled and butted.'

Ricky laughed. 'I heard about that. You hit him in the kidneys so hard he was pissing blood for two days.'

'So I've heard,' I said. 'But that crap's the last thing you need now.'

'Don't worry,' Norrie said. 'The first time he tries that,

he'll be on a train back to Glasgow. And he won't get paid a penny.' His tone was sharp. He didn't like anybody telling him anything. But hiring Tambourini was just stupid.

Ricky asked if I'd play chess with him. I didn't feel like it, but I'd promised the day before. 'Okay.'

The flat was habitable. There was a living room with a tiny kitchenette, two bedrooms and a bathroom. The living-room furniture looked as though it'd come from one of those second-hand shops that have fraudulent signs reading 'Antiques' over the doorway. Ricky and I lay on the tartan rug in front of the gas fire, with the chessboard between us. While we played, Norrie grilled some fish. I don't eat meat, so all I got was toasted cheese.

'You didn't sound too sure of yourself yesterday,' I said to Ricky.

'I'm okay,' he said. I didn't believe him. 'I'm always nervous, even when I know I'm definitely going to win.'

'You're definitely going to win this one,' Norrie called from the kitchenette. I wondered whether he believed it. I knew Ricky didn't.

I left around three. When I got back to my bedsit, I met one of my neighbours for the first time. He was in the kitchen, using the cooker, when I went in to fill my electric kettle. 'Hi,' he said, looking round from the congealing mess in the frying pan. 'You're the new guy.'

'I know.' I went to the sink and turned on the tap.

'Your name's Billy.'

I knew that, too. 'Uh-huh. What's yours?'

'Gordon.' He was about twenty, with Gothic clothes and the uniform dyed black hair. 'You a student?'

'No. I'm a journalist. What about you?'

'Student. At Edinburgh Uni.'

'This kitchen was in a hell of a state yesterday morning,' I said.

'That was Hugh, Patron Saint of Dirty Bastards. He used to live in the room next to yours.'

'He doesn't now?'

'Nah. Moved out yesterday afternoon. I finally drove him out. It was me that tidied the kitchen once he'd pissed off.'

'How'd you mean, drove him out?' I asked.

'I got fed up asking him to stop messing the kitchen. So I started pissing in his bathwater and using his toothbrush to clean the crapper.'

'What're the other tenants like? You're the first I've seen.'

'Until the landlord gets somebody else for Hugh's room, there's only one other. Brian. He's all right. You don't see much of him. Stays with his girlfriend most of the time.'

I went back to my room and made some tea, then tried to do some work. I wrote a few pages of notes, mostly about Ricky's nervousness. I have the notebook beside me right now. One passage reads:

I think his knowledge tells him he's unlikely to lose, but his gut tells him he's not going to win. That could be fatal. It's okay being terrified of losing, like being terrified of getting cancer or AIDS, as long as you don't really think it's going to happen, or at least think that it might not. Being scared of being beaten is fine; it can even help you avoid it. But expecting it to happen's different. If he thinks he'll lose, he will. I can understand why he feels like he does. He's never wanted anything but this. If he loses, he's probably as well dead. But he must shake it off. Cetera won't feel like that; he's champion already. And he'll punish Ricky for feeling like that. Cetera'll be afraid of being beaten, but he won't be expecting it to happen.

Ricky might freeze, or he might panic and go berserk. In either case, I don't forsee a happy ending. He's got to snap out of it, or it looks like being a win for Cetera on points (or even by late stoppage?).

The phone rang. I went out to the hall and answered it. 'Piers.'

'Hi.' It was Karen.

'Hi. I was going to phone you tonight,' I lied. Strangely, it was quite nice to hear her voice. 'How're things?' I asked, exploring new depths of inane conversation.

'All right.' She sounded bright enough. 'I phoned you twice last night.'

'Sorry. I was with Alan.'

'How's he?'

'Not so bad.' I am one *brilliant* conversationalist. 'He asked about you. Sends his lust.'

She laughed. 'Give him mine.'

Silence.

'Have you really been okay? No problems?' I asked. Atta-boy, Billy. Gloss it over. Don't say what you really mean. *Been nuts since I last saw you?*

'No, I've been fine. Honest. I actually feel quite good. I don't know why.'

Hey – wouldn't it be funny if Karen found she was much happier without you? Wouldn't it, Billy? Wouldn't you laugh? Wouldn't that be such a piss-case? Wouldn't you just LAUGH?

Ho, ho.

'I'm really missing you, though,' she added.

'I'm missing you.'

'So when can I come through and see you?'

'I don't know yet. I'm pretty busy. But we'll try to arrange it soon. I really do want to see you.' According to folk legend, Tam Pepper was cast out of hell for lying; I wouldn't even get in. 'But guess who's through here already?'

'Tell me.'

In a melodramatic, nasal tone, I began to recite. '*Ricky Mallon was a boxer man/who fought from Glasgow to Taiwan . . .*'

Karen sounded as though she was having a fit. 'I knew it!' she said through her laughter. '*Murdo!* I knew he'd show up!'

'Uh-huh. The bard of the lobotomy ward himself.'

'How'd he find you?'

'Fucked if I know. How's he always find us?' He'd even turned up when Ricky was training in Lagos, Nigeria. 'I haven't seen him yet. There was just this poem under Ricky's door this morning.'

'Let's hear the rest of it.'

'I haven't got it. That bit was just from memory. I'll get a copy from Ricky and send it through. Wait'll you see it – it's his worst ever.'

She laughed again. 'I can't wait. How's Ricky doing?'

'Not so good. He's really nervous about the fight.'

'That's natural.'

'Not this nervous, this early. If he doesn't get a grip, he'll be beaten before he's even in the ring.'

'Well, wish him luck from me,' she said. 'I met Liz in Byres Road today. She says Ricky won't see her till after the fight. She's upset.'

'I can imagine. But he's right.'

'Just as long as you're not planning the same thing. It'd better not be four weeks before I see you.'

'It won't be.' *Not unless I can think up a good excuse, anyway.* 'I'll ring you as soon as I've got some time.'

'Have you started to write?'

'Just notes. The sparring hasn't started yet, so there's nothing much to write about. The sparring partners're arriving tomorrow.' She'd have given birth if she'd known I'd been sparring with Ricky.

'I'd better go,' she said. 'I've got to ring Morag.'

'Okay. If you have any – bother, just pick up the phone. It doesn't matter what time it is.'

'Thanks. I will. Don't forget to send a copy of Murdo's poem.'

'I'll remember. 'Bye.'

'I love you.'

'I love you.' I hung up. I wondered what sort of poem Murdo'd have written if he'd known about Karen and me.

Billy wrote so well, he was transcendental/His lady suffered from problems that were mental . . .

I went to the takeaway downstairs and got a baked potato. After I'd eaten, I sat and played my guitar for a few hours. I wished Kerry'd phone. It was dark outside, and heavy rain was flaying the windows. I watched it for a long time. The city at night in the rain is like a beautiful song you know you'll never be able to sing or play properly.

I went to bed.

FOUR

For about a fortnight after the tender loving care I'd received from Victor Gezuli, I wondered what to do next. Every time I passed a fruit shop, I thought of what might have happened. So I decided to quit boxing.

You'd think that when you decide to quit the business you've devoted most of your teens and all your adult life to, it would come as a major event. But it didn't. I made up my mind on a Saturday afternoon when I was on my way to meet Alan. We went for a walk along the River Clyde walkway. It was a hot day in July and there was a lot of people about, families mostly.

'Guess what?' I said.

'Your period's late.'

'I'm not going to fight again.'

'Why not?'

'I like being in one piece.'

'Good. It's high time. You've been talking through your nose for a while now.'

'I know.' Others had noticed it.

'So what're you going to do now? Settle down and produce 2.2 sprogs?'

'Don't really know. There's nothing I'm qualified to do. I can see me having to spend some time in college. Or something.'

He laughed. 'I can just see you as a student! Doing what?'

'I don't know,' I admitted.

That night, I phoned my manager, Rab Edkin. 'Billy! How's my boy?' he said.

'Not so bad. Still breathing, anyway.'

'You gave us all a scare the other week. When you collapsed like that, I thought you were a goner.'

'I know. I didn't see it, didn't feel it. One minute I was fighting, the next the ref was helping me up.'

'Are you going to carry on fighting?'

'No. That one was enough.'

To my surprise, and slightly wounded pride, he approved. 'Good. What you got from Gezuli was a warning. You're right to take it. I mean, you're the bravest boy I've ever looked after. You've never let me down once. But you're just not hard enough to mix it with the top men. And you're twenty-two now. You can't hit and run all night like you could when you were eighteen. And you're only going to get slower. I'm glad you're getting out. You could really get hurt if you don't.'

So there it was. I felt a peculiar sense of relief. 'Don't lose touch,' said Rab, but I knew I would.

Having made the most important decision of my life, I didn't feel any different. For another week I just took things easy and thought. I'd quite a bit of money saved, so I decided to see some strange, exotic places and maybe catch some strange, exotic venereal diseases. I spent three months in North America with some people I knew there, then moved down to California and saw a few world title fights from the ringside. After a brief stay in New York, which I didn't like, I headed for France. While in Paris, I started to write.

I'd been a voracious reader since the age of about sixteen. Until then, I was only semi-literate (there are a few unkind editors who'd say little's changed). But, having started reading, I found I couldn't stop and for the next five years read just about anything I could get hold of. Books – fiction or non-fiction, it didn't matter – plays, essays, magazine articles. I was like a junkie. I didn't even like to go and *see* plays, just to read them. I even preferred reading song lyrics to listening to records.

When you're that obsessive, you're going to end up giving it a go yourself. So, in Paris, I did. Undaunted by the fact that I didn't even know what grammar was (I thought it was a type of school), I set about writing a novel. What I lacked in ability, I made up for in conceit. Just after starting, I ran out of money and had to live rough for a month before making my way back to Glasgow. In one way and another I got home without having to swim the Channel, still working fanatically on my book.

I crashed on Alan's sofa for a while, then found a bedsit in the West End. I liked the place, with its strange urban village atmosphere. My bedsit was pretty squalid, with hot and cold running mice, but I was seldom in it often enough to worry. In the evenings, following a spell on the dole, I worked in an off-licence in Byres Road. During the day, I'd sit in the Mitchell Library and write. I'd work on my book from eleven in the morning till five in the afternoon, then go to work in the off-licence. It was usually about ten-thirty by the time I got home.

About eight months after settling in the West End, my novel was almost finished. I was working in the off-licence one Friday night, and looking forward to finishing my book the next day, when three girls came into the shop. They were all quite pissed, and they were having a furious argument about religion. I gathered that one was an atheist and the other two were Catholics of the sort who're not sure about heaven, but certain about hell. I listened to their argument as I doled out their Bacardi, and thought about what they'd said for a long while after they'd gone.

I was still thinking about it next morning as I made my way to the library. I pushed the thought away as I started to write, but it wouldn't go. At one, I had lunch in the library cafeteria.

When I went back to my desk in the library, I put my unfinished book into my bag. Then, at the top of a sheet of A4, I wrote the heading:

The Gospel of God the Sick Bastard
(according to St Billy Piers)

I wrote for three-and-a-half hours without a pause. In that time I produced an essay that articulated the ideas about God that'd been buzzing like flies in my head since the night before.

One of the Bacardi Debating Society had said she'd read about the American Church of God the Indifferent, which believes that there is a God, but He doesn't give two fucks about us. I didn't agree with that, but I wasn't an atheist either. I had my own idea about God, and in that essay I developed it with a fluency that astonished me. I wrote that while I didn't accept the Christian idea of a loving, benevolent God, I couldn't believe things just happened at random. I suggested that the most realistic name for a church would be The Church of God the Sick Bastard. It was certain, I wrote, that if there were a supreme being then He/She/It must be a racist, sexist, classist, sadistic, sick bastard who delighted in the eternal torture of mankind . . .

I said it all in plain, tight prose. By the time I'd finished, I knew I'd finally found my voice, and my purple, nearly finished novel was going to have to be completely rewritten or just written off.

I went to bed that night with the feeling that I'd finally stopped drifting, finally stopped wasting my time. I hadn't yet learned to type, but next day I persuaded a neighbour to do it for me. On Monday morning I posted a copy of the essay to Gary Scott, founder and editor of the *City Review*, the hip and radical Glasgow magazine. Scott had been sued for libel three times, and had spent three months in prison for contempt of court. He was almost legendary around Glasgow for his willingness to publish what he liked, regardless of what the law – or anybody else – said.

On Wednesday I received a letter from Scott, calling the essay 'interesting' and asking me to come and see him. It was quite a formal letter, but he'd added: 'PS. What's your next essay called – "Buddha the Fat Bastard"?'

I went to the offices of the *City Review* as soon as I'd read the letter. I'd expected the place to be pretty up-market, but it turned out to be a run-down basement in the Gorbals. Scott was a cheerfully aggressive man in his twenties. He looked like Norman Bates, but I didn't tell him. When I left his office twenty minutes later, he'd agreed to publish the essay in the next issue of the *Review*, and his secretary had written me a cheque.

Two days after the article appeared, Scott told me he'd received over a hundred letters of complaint about it. 'That's what I like,' he said. 'It did my old heart good.' I joined the staff of the *Review* as a part-time writer, and held the job for nearly a year. I also published in other magazines, and Scott arranged for me to do a block-release course in journalism at Napier Polytechnic in Edinburgh.

Then I heard about the setting up of another, equally hip but far less radical, Glasgow magazine called *The Voice*. I applied to them for some work, and they offered me the job of deputy editor. I was surprised, but I shouldn't have been. In the past year my articles on boxing, politics and anything else I happened to have a casual opinion on had got me a considerable cult following in the city. So, with no hard feelings from Scott, I moved to *The Voice* and met Karen.

It was in an open-plan office in the West End. Apart from me, there were five full-time staff: Colin Glencross, the editor, Paul Gillespie, photographer, Angie Something-or-other, secretary, and Karen Fleming, graphic artist. *Mrs* Karen Fleming, I was disappointed to discover the first time I saw the staff list. Not that I objected to twenty-year-old, very talented girls being married – just the gorgeous ones like her.

And not that her being married stopped us from flirting from the moment we met. I used to delight in trying to shock her, and never succeeded.

'Fancy some tea?' she'd ask.

'No. How about sex, though?' I'd say.

'Pardon?'

'Fancy going halfers on a baby?'

'Not right now, thanks,' she'd say. 'If I do, I'll make sure you're the first to know.' Not at all thrown; I wondered if she was used to such proposals.

The Voice got off to a reasonable start, which was entirely owing to the work Glencross and I put into it. Deadline for the first issue was 3 April. On 31 March we were about a fortnight behind schedule, and almost shitting ourselves. For both of us, it was our first journalistic job of real responsibility, and we were terrified of fucking up.

For three days, we worked eighteen hours a day. We wrote and edited our own articles, and edited all the stuff by our part-time writers. We sent the copy to the typesetters, and when the proofs came back we sat up all night in the office and read them. On the evening of 2 April we sat over layout sheets and got down to the excruciating business of layout and paste-up, which is like doing the Rubik cube, only worse. At five o'clock on the morning of 3 April, the magazine was ready. Holding it as if it was made of crystal, we got into the office car and drove to our printers in Alloa. By noon the magazine was on the streets and selling, and I was in bed and sleeping. I didn't wake for eighteen hours.

When I did wake, it was with the vague realisation that Karen was pregnant. Following our trip to the printers, Glencross and I had made a brief visit to the magazine office, just to say we were going home for some sleep and they could expect us back when they saw us. We got there at just after nine, and Karen was the only one in the office.

She grinned at us from behind her desk as we came in. Glencross was fresher than me. I was so tired I could barely see properly. 'You look smug,' Glencross told her as I fell into a chair.

'Uh-huh. I've got some bad news for Billy.' She looked at me for a reaction, but I just squinted at her dopily.

'What news is that?' Glencross asked.

She looked at me. 'Remember I said I'd tell you if I wanted a baby? Well, I forgot.'

Glencross and I went through all the motions of delighted congratulation, but I was too exhausted to be sincere. But when I woke, I phoned her home to congratulate her properly. There was no answer, which shouldn't have surprised me on a Saturday night.

I was late for work on Monday morning. I'd been up late, working on the soon-to-be-abandoned rewrite of my novel. Now that I had a job to do during the day, I no longer wrote in the Mitchell Library. I'd moved to a slightly less squalid (ie no mice) bedsit in Clarence Drive, and most nights I wrote there.

'On time as usual,' said Karen as I came in. Glencross was out on a story or something, and there was nobody else in the office. Karen was at her desk, working on some drawings.

I hung up my coat and sat at my desk. 'Slept in again. I sat up writing most of the night.' I looked at her. She wore black jeans and a tight blue jumper, and there was no change in her figure. 'Was I hallucinating on Friday, or are you really pregnant?'

'I'm really pregnant.'

'Mm. I like kids. Used to go to school with them,' I told her. 'You don't look any fatter.'

'I shouldn't for a while yet.'

'How'd it happen?'

'Brian kissed me, then we took our clothes off . . .'

'I mean, I didn't think you planned to have a kid.'

'I planned to eventually, but not this soon,' she said. 'But it seems the pill doesn't work on me.'

'How come?'

'Don't know. It doesn't work with everybody. I've been pregnant before.'

'What? When?'

'Last year. I miscarried. My womb wasn't strong enough to hold the baby.'

'So what about this time?'

'The doctor's given me some exercises to strengthen my womb. He says it should be all right.'

'Good . . . I hope so.'

'So do I. But I know it will. I can just feel it. If anything was going to go wrong, I'd know.'

For the rest of that week, Glencross and I hardly let her do a stroke of work. When she came down with a slight cold on Friday, we insisted – to her exasperation – that she take the following week off.

'I'm *fine*,' she protested. 'It's just a *cold*.'

'Take the week off. We won't need you for ages yet, anyway,' said Glencross.

'I'll be bored out of my skull. Brian's going on a fishing trip. I'll be on my own.'

'You can watch the afternoon kids' programmes,' I said. 'You're as well getting used to it.'

She gave in, but when we insisted on getting a taxi to take her home, she almost hit us. But she was pleased by the attention. Pity she had to be married, I thought as her gorgeous figure disappeared into the cab.

Over the weekend, Glencross phoned me twice with the news that sales of our first issue seemed to be satisfactory, though not spectacular. He'd phoned both John Menzies and W. H. Smith. Both said the mag was selling, though – despite our advertising campaign – it wasn't attracting the same number of readers who bought Gary Scott's *City Review*. That didn't surprise me; I knew Scott's was the better magazine. If *The Voice* was to survive in the long term, we'd have to adopt a brave and aggressive editorial policy similar to his. In the end, that just didn't happen.

We spent the next Monday and Tuesday sitting in the office and planning the contents of the next issue. It was clear to me even then that Glencross's view of the shape the mag should take was a lot different from mine. His vision was essentially square. I accused him of wanting another *Church Times*, and he retorted – wrongly – that all I wanted was a shock sheet. As editor, he got his way, but I think the conclusion proved me right. *The Voice* would last for more than a year, but it constantly lost money and ultimately couldn't survive in a Scottish market dominated by the fearless *City Review*. After issue fourteen, it folded.

We argued furiously all of Tuesday morning, then Glencross growled that he was going for lunch and stamped out. Not long after he'd gone Karen came in.

'Oh, hi –' I began, then stopped as I got a real look at her.

The expression on her face as she looked at me bore the same resemblance to a smile as a tailor's dummy bears to a living person. She looked ill. Her face actually looked *thick*. It seemed bloated and shapeless. Some spots I'd never noticed before now stood out against the pale skin. She was like a diseased Barbie doll.

'Hi, Billy.' She didn't sound too good, either. She sat down at her desk without taking off her coat.

'I thought you were having the week off,' I said. She didn't answer, just started flipping through the sheets of paper on her desk. 'Are you all right?' I asked stupidly.

'No. I don't think so.' It wasn't the voice of a living person. It reminded me of the flat hum of a TV set after closedown. It was a noise, not a voice. 'I've lost my baby. Lost it.'

'Oh, Jesus.' I went to her as she rose from the chair, and held her as she began to cry. She didn't cry like an adult, but in the raging helpless manner of a hysterical child. Her face was buried in my chest, and I could feel tears, snot and saliva soaking through my shirt. I stroked her hair, unable to say anything that wouldn't have been stupid. Both of us shook with the force of her crying.

After a while, her crying stopped as suddenly as it'd begun. She removed her face from my chest and eyed the soaking shirt and tie. 'Sorry. Got a hanky?'

I dug one out of my jacket pocket and gave it to her. She blew her nose twice. 'Sorry,' she said again. Her voice sounded a bit more human now.

I hugged her. 'Don't talk crap. The shirt needed a wash, anyway. Set me back 50p in Paddy's Market.' She tried a smile and nearly made it.

'I just came in for something to do,' she said. 'Brian's away fishing. He won't be back till Thursday or Friday. I couldn't sit on my own.'

'Of course you couldn't. But you're not doing any work. If I take the afternoon off, d'you fancy going for a drink or something?' I didn't think the atmosphere between Glencross and me'd be too pleasant for her.

'Okay,' she said. 'I don't mind.'

When I heard Glencross's footsteps coming up the stairs, I went out and waylaid him in the corridor. Quickly, I told him what'd happened and asked if I could have the afternoon off to look after her.

'Yeah.' He looked shocked. 'Yeah ... Of course you can ...'

'Thanks, Colin.'

'Thanks, nothing. Is she all right?'

'Would you be?'

'I'd better go and say sorry or something, then you can get going. Take care of her.'

'I'll do what I can.' I waited in the corridor while he went into the office. A few minutes later, Karen came out. She was carrying my overcoat. I took it from her. 'Okay?'

'Not okay. Better,' she said. 'Where're we going?'

'Wherever you like.'

'I don't mind. I don't know the West End.' She lived in Riddrie, on the East side of the city.

'How about O'Henry's?'

'All right.'

O'Henry's Café-Bar was built into an old railway arch under Kelvinbridge. The setting was leafy and idyllic, with the River Kelvin flowing just a few feet from the front door. The place was quiet when we arrived. Karen sat at a table near the door, and I went up to the bar. I ordered brandy for her – she normally drank Bacardi, but I'd heard somewhere that brandy was good for you if you'd had a shock – and Guinness for myself.

Karen sipped her brandy, and if she noticed it wasn't Bacardi she didn't mention it. 'I really didn't think I'd lose it this time. I felt okay. I knew it was going to happen last time. I could *feel* it. But this time I felt *okay*.'

I just held her hand. I couldn't begin to think of anything to say.

'And the doctor says Brian'll have to have a vasectomy or I'll have to be sterilised.'

'Why?' I said ingeniously.

'The doctor says I'm lucky I miscarried so early. If I get pregnant again and manage to hold it a bit longer, it could kill me.'

'Why weren't you able to carry it?' I asked. Then, realising that it probably wasn't the best time to indulge my morbid curiosity, I added, 'If you don't want to talk about it, don't worry . . .'

'I got raped when I was nine. It seems to have made quite a mess of my insides. It certainly hasn't done my womb much good.'

I don't remember what I said. It was probably the usual my-God-that's-terrible routine. Karen showed no self-pity, then or ever. In the future, on the few occasions she talked about the rape, she talked about it casually, and sometimes with black humour. Before the start of her illness, I only had one indication of how badly scarred she still was. It was one morning after she'd left my flat, having stayed the night with me. Beside the bed I'd left a copy of the *New Statesman*, on top of some other magazines and newspapers. It'd been lying there for weeks and I'd forgotten all about it. But, that morning, I noticed that Karen'd turned it face down. For some reason, I habitually left *all* my magazines face up. So I turned it over, and saw that this particular issue had dealt with child abuse. The cover had a photo of the sort of dolls, with genitals, used to help victims explain what'd happened to them. The sort they'd used in Karen's case.

But, that afternoon in O'Henry's, all that was in the future. And it'd be a long time before I'd tell Karen what'd happened to me when *I* was nine. And before.

We stayed in O'Henry's till about eight in the evening. I stayed on the Guinness, but Karen switched to orange juice after her third brandy. We talked and I was shown a picture of her life, past and present, that was different to the one I'd imagined from our casual banter in the office.

She'd been married nearly two years. She was now twenty and her husband was sixteen years older. He was unable to work, owing to a back injury caused by a heavy stepladder falling on him some years before. The doctors said the injury would gradually worsen and eventually lead to a wheelchair. For the time being, he could live normally as long as he steered clear of heavy labour. This didn't apply to punching Karen, which, I was to discover, he was able to manage quite regularly.

They'd met when she was seventeen. He was a friend of her father's, and visited the house regularly. Her parents, particularly her mother, had made her live like a recluse since she was nine. She'd go to school, come home, and that was all. She'd had no friends and, at seventeen, had never had a boyfriend. One boy had asked her for a date when she was fifteen. She'd told him she'd like to, but would have to ask her mother. Her mother's response was to send her off to stay with relatives in Greece for nearly a year. So, when her imbecile alcoholic father's imbecile alcoholic friend Brian Fleming took a fancy to her, it was decided to have a wedding.

Karen didn't object. She didn't know enough about anything to want to object.

Her drongo husband really landed on his feet. Being married to a child who'd been brought up to do nothing but cook and clean, he could now give up sitting around drinking in squalor and take up sitting around drinking in comfort. They lived in a council flat in Riddrie, which he'd shared with a previous wife till she'd come to her senses and left him. Life was pretty settled. He'd drink, she'd cook and once a fortnight they'd go to the dole and sign on. They sometimes fucked, too.

But, somewhere along the line, Karen discovered she could draw, and draw exceptionally well. She began earning a few extra pounds by doing charcoal portraits of her neighbours' babies, dogs, goldfish and anything else they might want to hang on the wall. That led to a night class, which led to the end of her almost pathological shyness. That led to her drawings being used by various magazines, which led her to working for *The Voice*. That was to lead to other things.

I spent a lot of time with her in the couple of days following her miscarriage. In fact, I took her with me everywhere I went: to bookshops, libraries, to visit the mag's advertisers to try to persuade them to advertise with us again. I knew how to show a girl a good time.

Then her husband returned from his fishing trip, and she was off work for a couple of weeks. We assumed she needed to be alone with him for a while. The truth was that he'd got drunk and knocked fuck out of her. When she came back to work, she seemed her old amiable, sarcastic self.

'Something for you,' she said to me just before she left at five. Glencross and I were going to work all night again; deadline for issue two was approaching. Karen tossed a blue envelope onto my desk. 'See you tomorrow,' she called as she left.

Glencross, whose desk was next to mine, looked curious but didn't say anything. We weren't getting along at all well by that time. 'Back in a minute,' I said. I went to the bog and opened the envelope.

It contained a handmade card. On the front, she'd drawn a picture of a swan in a rain-lashed pond. Inside, she'd written:

Thanks for being around when I needed somebody.

She'd signed it *Love, me*. Much later, she'd tell me that she'd been tempted to leave out the comma.

It took a few more months for me to realise she fancied me. And I only realised when she told me. I wouldn't recognise a hint if it came up and buggered me in broad daylight. But, most of the time, I was just too busy to take much notice of her. The casual flirting in the office went on, though I didn't make any more jokes about going halfers on a baby. But Glencross and I were working a sixty-hour week, sometimes more, to try to keep the magazine afloat. I'd already be in the office and working on something when Karen arrived in the morning. I'd work all day, sometimes skipping lunch, and usually at some point I'd suggest copulation to her, she'd agree, and I'd carry on working. I'd still be working when she went home. Glencross once remarked that I seemed to make her forget she was married. I laughed and said I wouldn't mind if she forgot completely, but I was joking and thought he was too.

After the fifth issue of *The Voice* came out, things got a bit more organised. We'd made our contacts and knew who was certain to advertise with us. The pressure was still intense, but we were able to work at a slightly saner pace. I didn't have much time for a social life, though. I saw a bit of Alan, and sometimes met Gary Scott for a drink. I had a few short (one only lasted two days) relationships with women who got shot of me in favour of guys who had time actually to see them once in a while.

The last of these had just given me the push, and I told Karen about it over lunch. She surprised me by saying, 'She needs her head examined.'

'Eh?'

'I'll tell you something. If I wasn't married, I'd be after you myself.'

I asked if she was joking, but only for something to say. I knew she wasn't. I also knew – the way you just *know* – that her being married wouldn't make any difference unless I let it.

So I decided to let it. I'd more than enough on my plate.

For the next couple of weeks, I avoided being on my own with her. I stopped going for lunch with her unless I knew someone else was going to be there. Not that I expected to be raped in a café or pub; it was myself I didn't trust.

Everyone had to work late one night to meet the deadline for issue seven. We knocked off at nine in the evening, and Glencross invited us all for a drink. So nine-fifteen found Glencross, Karen, Paul Gillespie, our photographer, Angie Something, our secretary, and me sitting in O'Henry's. It was a humid summer night, and our table was near the open door. Karen wore a floral-patterned skirt and top. She had her hair swept back and up in a way that made her look like one of those Greek statues. She was talking mostly to Glencross, but she was sitting next to me.

By ten-thirty, we'd put away more than is good for your liver, and were all feeling pretty much at one with ourselves. Karen, who usually didn't drink much, was red in the face and finding the most inane of our jokes uproariously funny. Sometimes, as she laughed at something I'd said, she'd pat me on the thigh. I noticed she never did it to anyone else.

I felt excited and worried. I didn't say much, just listened through a pleasant drunken haze to what the others were saying. Glencross was telling us he was considering writing a book about deprivation and violence in Glasgow's housing schemes, particularly Easterhouse, where Karen'd been brought up. I heard him say something about what violence can lead to, and mention boxing, and Karen looked at me and Paul said something about my having been a boxer, and I found myself thinking, as I always tried not to, about my first time.

It happened, as most people's probably does, at primary school. Davie Kelly, I remember his name was. I sometimes wonder what happened to him. Nothing good, I hope. At my primary school in Possil, arguably the filthiest slum area in Glasgow at the time, every class had its Best Fighter, usually just the strongest, best-developed little thug in the class. The most hallowed title was that of Best Fighter in the School, who could expect to have his arse kissed until it shone.

The Best Fighter in primary seven, the most senior class, was usually Best Fighter in the School unless, as occasion sometimes had it, the Best Fighter in primary six happened to be unusually good. When I was eight years old, Davie Kelly was the Best Fighter in our class, and looked likely to attain the coveted position of Best Fighter in the School long before he reached primary six or seven. A dark, squat, grunting little monster who made Prince Vlad the Impaler look like an all-right guy, he had already been suspended from school for breaking a kid's collarbone; pretty hot going for an eight-year-old. I, in total contrast, was legendary for my cowardice, and probably held the unofficial title of Worst Fighter in the Class. Not really fair, considering that I'd never really been in a fight. Nearly everybody had pushed me around at one time or another – even some of the girls, one of whom was more man than I'll ever be – but I'd always just accepted it rather than let it lead to a fight. Anyway, Kelly seemed to regard specky, skinny, shitbag Piers as being too unimportant to be worth murdering, and – believe me – I could live with that.

But Master Kelly had a devoted shadow, an evil, crawling little Iago called Sneader. And one afternoon, for no reason I know of, this stinking little fuckpig decided that I was in need of his friend's tender loving care. The word spread through the class that specky skinny shitbag Piers was in for it, but the said specky skinny shitbag was not informed. So, in blessed ignorance of my impending dismantling, I was crossing the playground at four o'clock when about half of my class descended on me and I was dragged to the shed at the back of the school, where their master was waiting.

One of the reasons that I'm a vegetarian is that I once visited a slaughterhouse, and saw the terror a cow experienced *before* the killing started. It was as though the animal sensed the obscene ritual it was about to be put through. And as I looked at the cow I sympathised, because I felt sure that I knew its fear. I'd suffered the same dizzy terror that day, twelve years before, when I was dragged across the concrete floor of the shed to face Davie Kelly. I knew for the first time what it was to be afraid – not nervous, not worried, but truly *afraid*.

The assembled audience was silent as Kelly looked at me with all the intelligence of a cancer cell. 'Did you ca' me a poof, ya wee cunt?' he demanded.

'Naw,' I squeaked truthfully. Had it ever occurred to me to question Kelly's sexuality, I wouldn't have whispered it in the middle of an empty field in case it somehow got back to him.

'Aye, he fuckin' did! Ah heard him!' proclaimed Sneader, and my fate was sealed.

'Ah'm gauny knock fuck oot ye!' Kelly told me. 'Yer gettin' yer specky wee face kicked in!'

I tried to speak, to plead, could not, then tried again. And then, to my horror, I heard myself say, in a voice that shook, 'Here's the face – where's the courage?'

At my words, I nearly fainted and Kelly ran out of conversation. He swung a right that connected firmly with its target, and my specky wee face, though it remained wee, was no longer specky. I hit the floor before my glasses did. I sat on the cold, damp concrete and watched as they shattered against the far wall.

The next I remember, Kelly and I were on the far side of the shed and my hands were aching. With some surprise I realised that this was because I was hitting them against Kelly's head. Hard. And if I was surprised, Kelly wasn't exactly taking it in his stride either. He hit back once or twice and the blows landed, but they didn't hurt and I battered him mercilessly with both hands. Not a sound came from his disciples. It was like fighting in a morgue, which was probably where they'd expected me to end up.

Kelly's hands were down and he was obviously finished. Tough shit. I wasn't. I continued to hammer away, raining blows now on his big hard body as well as his greasy, shaggy head. He dropped heavily to his knees, and I heard myself speak again.

'You broke my glasses, you fucking bastard,' I sobbed. Then, with an eight-year-old's strict observance of Queensberry Rules, I hauled off and kicked his head with all my might. He fell over on to his side, totally unconscious. I bent, rolled him on to his back and sat on his chest.

Behind me, I could hear Sneader crying, saying 'Somebody get a teacher.' I looked down at Kelly's face. It was grey, and blood was trickling from both nostrils.

'Billy – ' I heard someone say.

'Fuck off.' I continued to look at Kelly's face, hypnotised by the blood. When it stopped, I slapped his nose and it began again. At that, the onlookers scattered. *Oh they didn't like the show now oh no not one little bit –*

I don't remember the rest all that well now. The others came back with some teachers who sent Kelly to hospital and took me home to tell my parents I was to be suspended from school. After the teachers left, my mother meted out the punishment I always received for not looking after my glasses; she removed my trousers and held a match to my balls for a few seconds.

'Are you all right, Billy?' Karen had stopped talking to Glencross and was looking at me with concern.

I smiled, feeling the memories pour away from me like piss you've been holding in for hours. 'Fine,' I said easily.

'I thought you were going to be sick. You looked terrible.'

'I'm okay. I was just thinking about something a bit . . . sick.'

She smiled at me. 'I believe it.' I wasn't surprised when she took my hand under the table and squeezed it.

Later that night, Karen and I were in a taxi on the way to my bedsit. 'Did you know before?' she asked me. We were holding hands.

'Uh-huh. I was pretty sure. I didn't want to cause a mess.'

'Will it?'

'I hope not,' I said. 'But we're going to have to have a talk. Tomorrow.'

'I know.' She leaned against me, the warmth of the cab making her sleepy. 'But we shouldn't tonight.'

'We won't. But we will tomorrow.'

She didn't answer. She was nearly asleep. I nudged her gently as the taxi stopped outside my close. She squirmed slightly and mumbled something. Her skirt had ridden up to a maddening height. I nudged her again and she came fully awake, sitting up and blinking drowsily at me. She looked about twelve years old.

I ruffled her hair. 'We're here.' I helped her out of the taxi and paid the driver. Then we went upstairs. As I unlocked the door to my bedsit, I thought about what'd happened to her when she was a kid. I knew I mustn't push. If she changed her mind, or wanted to stop, I had to take no for an answer.

I put a lamp on. Karen sat on the single bed and looked around. It was a small room, made smaller by the clutter. The walls were covered with posters and photocopies of articles I'd published. It probably wasn't what she'd expected and it certainly wasn't what she was used to.

She yawned, and stretched her legs out from the bed. 'Mind if I take my shoes off?'

'I don't mind what you take off.' I sat down next to her and put an arm around her shoulder. We kissed, gently at first, then with increasing passion. I shivered, half with excitement, half with nervousness, as I felt her tongue push into my mouth. When we broke the kiss, her face was scarlet and her eyes bright.

She slid a hand inside my shirt. Her touch felt warm and assured. 'Want to make love to me?' she breathed.

'Mm . . . Now that you mention it . . .' I kissed her long and deeply, and helped her off with her top. She wasn't wearing a bra. I threw the top on to a chair. She lay on her back, smiling self-consciously. Her body was firm, her breasts large. I bent over and kissed them each in turn, watching the nipples erect as she stroked my hair. She lay still as I removed her skirt, her tights and, finally, her knickers.

For a few seconds I sat on the edge of the bed and just looked at her. The hair between her legs was thick and dark. I reached for her and caressed her wet heat with my fingers. She whimpered softly and wriggled.

I stood up and tore off my shirt, trousers and everything else that's commonly torn off at such moments. I lay down beside her and I was so hard I thought I might come if she so much as touched me. I didn't dare penetrate her, knowing that the pill didn't work on her and she hadn't yet been sterilised. I knew I had some condoms somewhere, but I wasn't going to spend the rest of the night looking for them.

I put a hand between her legs and began rubbing slowly. She spread her legs wide to let me reach deeper. I rubbed faster, kissing her breasts as I did. She was moaning like she was trying out for Scottish Opera. My hand was as wet as it would've been if I'd held it under a tap. She came so hard I thought I'd have to scrape her off the ceiling.

I held her, her face pressed against my neck. '*That was so good.*' She was almost sobbing, shuddering violently. Then she was still. We lay and kissed for a while, then she said, 'Tell me what you like.'

I couldn't, though I knew what I wanted. 'What do *you* like?' I countered.

She smiled. 'You'll be surprised, but I don't know. This is the first time I've ever enjoyed it.' It did surprise me, but I believed her.

Without warning, she moved down and pillowed her head on my groin. I gasped as her tongue flicked lightly at my cock, and I heard her ask, 'Is it all right?'

'Uh-huh.'

And then it was like I was drowning in her, and everything was as you always hope it will be but it usually isn't.

That was the start of it.

FIVE

'Something, isn't it?' said Ricky Mallon. We'd just climbed Arthur's Seat, the famous hill just outside Edinburgh. We'd had a race to get to the top, and of course Ricky'd won.

I sat slumped against the stone marker that lets you know you're at the peak. Ricky, who wasn't even breathing heavily, stood leaning on it.

'Yeah.' The view was spectacular. It was four o'clock on a clear afternoon, and we could see right across Edinburgh. The city had a shimmering beauty that no city really has.

'What d'we do now?' said Ricky. 'Sit and look at it?' He was joking, but it wasn't funny. I got my breath and stood up.

'We get going before that sweat dries and you catch your death,' I told him. We were wearing tracksuits and hiking boots.

'I'm hardly sweating at all,' he said as we started downhill. 'It's pissing off you.'

'I know. It's fucking pathetic. I used to be able to run ten times the distance, twice as fast.'

'So what happened?'

'It's called Guinness,' I said.

We walked carefully over the wet and bumpy terrain till we reached the road that led down to the city. Then we began to jog.

'How's your hand?' I asked.

'Fine. Not a twinge.' He held out his left hand and wiggled the fingers. One of the knuckles was noticeably swollen.

'Told you Tambourini could hurt you.'

He laughed. 'I feel a bit rotten about it.'

Earlier that day, my warning about hiring Steve Tambourini as a sparring partner had been proven right. But what'd happened seemed to have done Ricky some good.

It'd been Tambourini's first – and, it turned out, last – day in Edinburgh. I went to have a shower as Ricky started in with the other sparmate, Chris Moyer. Moyer was so punchy he was almost a simpleton, but he was a nice enough guy. He was a strong, hustling fighter, similar to the world champion in style. He had little punching power, but he could soak up punishment.

I showered and went back into the gym to watch. Ricky and Moyer were still at it. Supervised by Norrie, they were working close in, Ricky banging in short, wicked hooks to the body.

Tambourini was standing on the ring apron, wearing gloves and a headguard. We didn't say anything to each other. He was about the biggest pain in the arse ever to hold a pro fighter's licence. He was in his late twenties, and his behaviour would've embarrassed a twelve-year-old. He wasn't really that bad a guy; that'd be giving him too much credit. He was just a nasty child. I don't think his reason for fighting dirty even in sparring was that he liked hurting people (you can do that without breaking a single rule). I think he just liked doing what he wasn't supposed to.

Ricky had a habit of grunting and snorting as he punched. Each time he grunted as he hit Moyer, Tambourini would grunt loudly along with him. It didn't seem to annoy Ricky, but after a while Norrie snapped, 'Fuck's sake, Steve. Grow up.' Tambourini fell into a sulky silence.

Ricky seemed all right. The three-minute rounds were timed by a clock on the wall, which rang a bell at the start and finish of each round. As soon as the first bell rang, Ricky'd be after Moyer, weaving, crowding, moving inside and punching all the time. He wasn't trying to hurt Moyer. He just swarmed all over him, outpunching him four for one. Norrie looked on, giving occasional instructions.

'Balance, Ricky. Watch the balance. Don't lunge . . . That's it, up the middle . . . Careful with the heads, both of you . . . Make him work, Chris. Be first. That's it. Nice.'

I wondered how long Ricky could sustain such a demented pace. What if Cetera wouldn't fall under such an onslaught?

The bell rang. 'That'll do, Chris,' said Norrie. 'Out you get. In, Steve.' Moyer looked thankful as he got out of the ring. I helped him take off his gloves and headguard. His face was scarlet, and steam rose from his sweaty body. He went for a shower, and I watched Ricky spar with Tambourini.

Tambourini could box. He had a side-on, classical style that made it hard to get a clear shot at his chin. As you came at him he'd jab you hard, move, and jab you twice more. His hand speed was blinding. It was only the lack of a real knockout punch that'd stopped him becoming a champion.

He was the sort of fighter Ricky found it hardest to cope with. But, as they sparred, Ricky was well in control. He stuck to his work and went after Tambourini relentlessly, refusing to be disheartened by the hit-and-run tactics. He had to take a lot of jabs, but he got in some good body shots.

Norrie was silent throughout the first round. 'Nice boxing, both of you,' he said when the bell rang. Tambourini stood in his corner, while Ricky prowled in a circle, looking at the floor. 'More of the same,' Norrie ordered as the bell rang again.

The second round was more punishing. In the final minute, Ricky's body punches took their toll, and Tambourini began to slow down. He stood more square-on than usual, and tried to fight Ricky off with a series of hooks to the head. Ricky took them without wobbling, then moved inside and hammered at Tambourini's body. Tambourini took it well. He managed to move away and get his jab to work. The pace was furious when the bell rang.

Ricky was turning to walk to his corner when Tambourini jabbed him once more for good measure. Before Norrie could say a word, Ricky had brought over a bludgeoning left hook. It got Tambourini on the side of the jaw, and he went down as if he'd been shot. He twitched a few times, then was still.

'Christ!' Norrie bent over and pulled Tambourini's gum-shield from his mouth.

'*He fucking hit me after the bell!*' Ricky looked like an angry, guilty child.

'I know,' I said. I got into the ring and turned him away from Tambourini. I unlaced his gloves and unfastened his headguard. 'Go and have a shower.'

'It wasn't – He hit me – ' He was scared.

'I know. You're not to blame. Go,' I said. He went. 'Is he dead?' I asked Norrie. He was cradling Tambourini's head in his lap and looking like he'd just died himself.

'No. I thought he was. But he's breathing.' Tambourini began to shake, and he retched. Norrie turned him on his side, and a small amount of vomit came out of his mouth. His face was actually green. I'd seen it before, death trying to take a young body that wasn't ready for it. I wondered if we should get an ambulance. Then Tambourini's eyelids began to flicker, and I went to my bag to get my shorthand notebook.

'You've nothing to feel rotten about,' I told Ricky as we jogged down from Arthur's Seat. 'He got what he asked for. It's your hand I'm worried about.' Ricky and Tambourini'd both gone to hospital, Tambourini with concussion and Ricky with a bruised left hand. Tambourini had then got on a train back to Glasgow, after wishing Ricky a brain haemorrhage during his fight.

'I told you, the hand's fine,' Ricky said as we ran. 'At least I know I can still put them on their backs. Tambourini's never been stopped before.'

He was right. Tambourini'd never even been on the floor. Neither had Cetera.

'You'll find Cetera easier to hit than Tambourini,' I said. 'But he's a lot more dangerous.'

'Uh-huh. I'm dangerous too.' His nervousness seemed to have been cured. 'Is your second's licence still current?'

'No. Why?' I used to hold a licence to second boxers, but I never used it and when it lapsed I didn't bother to renew it.

'You'd get another easy enough. I was thinking, I'd like you in the corner on the night. You could give Norrie a hand.'

'Forget it.'

'How come?'

'I'd be a liability. I'm no second. I know that from helping in people's corners while they sparred. You've only got a minute to do everything, and it gets me flustered. I'd still be cleaning your gumshield or fumbling for the waterbottle when the next round started.'

'I'd feel a lot better if you were there.'

'I'll *be* there,' I said. 'I'll be about as close to the ring as your seconds. You'll fucking *hear* me.'

The road down from the hill led us into Newington, where my bedsit was. We slowed to a walking pace. Ricky was feeling high, but a melancholy had been following me all the way down, and now it caught me. The city we were in bore no resemblance to the shimmering fairy-tale city I'd seen from the hill. I looked back at Arthur's Seat, and it looked as beautiful as it always does when you're not near it.

Ricky'd come in Norrie's car, which was parked outside my bedsit. 'Want to come up?' I asked him.

'Nah,' he said, and I was pleased. 'I'm knackered. I just want to have dinner and get to bed.' He got into the car. 'See you tomorrow?'

'Yeah.' I watched as he drove off, then went upstairs.

I sat at my desk and tried to do some work. I'd written down details of the incident in the gym in shorthand, with good quotes from Ricky and Norrie. Tambourini hadn't felt chatty. I'd phoned Ghengis Perring at the *Glasgow Clarion*, and he'd asked me to write up a report and phone it in the next day.

I stared at the blank sheet of A4 in my typewriter. I wanted Kerry. I imagined what it'd be like if I was writing this article at home just eight months earlier. Karen'd be out with Morag or somebody, and I'd be sitting at my desk by the window, just like I was now, and the doorbell'd ring and I'd answer it and it'd be Kerry.

Suddenly, I could imagine it so clearly. She'd be standing there on my doorstep, all blonde, gorgeous, six feet of her. 'Busy?' she'd ask. 'Or d'you fancy a cup of tea?'

'Busy, yeah. But a break won't kill me.' I'd follow her into her flat next door.

'What're you writing about?' she'd ask me.

As I sat at my desk and fantasised, I found myself starting to answer out loud. 'Ricky knocked a guy out in sparr – ' I broke off with a start, realising what I was doing. *Whee*, I thought. *So this is how it happens. Move over, Karen. And you thought you were the only one. Maybe they'll put us in the same padded cell. You won't have to worry about me leaving you then, will you? Come and get me, Doc. Gagagagagaga –*

I had to get out. 'Whatever happens, don't call me,' Kerry'd said. 'I need to get my head straight. Unless it's an emergency, don't call me.'

I decided to call her.

The phone in the hall only took incoming calls, but there was a call box just along the road. I went there, taking my shorthand notebook with me. I'd call Kerry, then go over to Alan's and stay the night there. I'd write the report for Perring on his typewriter.

I shivered, not knowing whether it was just the cold that was doing it. It was seven in the evening, so I knew she'd be home from work. I opened the address book I always kept in my jacket pocket. With the English dialling code, the Shropshire number was long and I nearly chickened out halfway through. Then the phone was picked up and a female voice that wasn't Kerry's said, 'Hello?'

'Hi. Can I speak to Kerry, please?'

'She's not back from Glasgow yet. Can I take a message?'

'*Where?*' I said stupidly.

'Glasgow. She went up the other day. For an interview. She'll be on her way back now. Can I take a message? Get her to call you back?'

'No. It's all right. Thanks.' I put the phone down.

She'd been back in Glasgow and hadn't got in touch. Just an hour's train journey away. That can't have been my only thought as I walked over to Alan's, but it's the only one I could remember afterwards.

Alan wasn't in. There was a pub close by, and I went in, knowing there was a pretty good chance he'd be there. He wasn't.

It was quite a nice pub, smart without being plush. It was busy, but not mobbed. I sat at the bar and ordered a pint of Guinness. I opened my notebook, put it on the bar and began to read over my notes.

'Is that Pitman's?' asked the barmaid. I looked up at her. She was plump and dark-haired, in her late twenties and friendly.

'No, it's Teeline,' I told her, forcing a smile so I'd seem taciturn rather than rude. I looked back down at my note-book.

'Looks difficult,' she said. I smiled and nodded, but didn't answer and didn't look up. She took the hint and said no more to me. I drank my Guinness and gazed at my notes, as though they might turn into an article. They didn't.

Another barmaid appeared, and the two of them started discussing a friend of theirs who'd been raped. From the bits I overheard, I gathered she'd been walking in Edinburgh's notorious Meadows when someone had stabbed her in the kidney with a screwdriver, pushed her down and raped her.

I couldn't take it. I downed my pint, ordered another, and went and sat at a table. I thought that if I drank much more I'd probably cry, and didn't know if that would be good. There was a couple sitting at the table I chose. I hoped they wouldn't talk to me and they didn't.

I stared at my notebook for a bit longer, then turned to a fresh page and got out my pen. Not sure what I was doing, but half drunk on less than two pints, I started to write in shorthand. I'm looking at it right now. I wrote:

I know I'm not perfect; a bit pathetic, even. But being like I am is all that gets me through. It really gets hard to laugh sometimes. I wish you loved me. I love you. I know I could be different if you loved me and my loving you didn't hurt anybody. It'd take time, and I'd never shake the past off entirely. But we could be happy, if I had some luck. I get scared sometimes. I love you. If you loved me, I'd try to give you so much. You know I could always make you smile.

I'd a few more pints, but while I'd managed to get pissed on a couple, I couldn't seem to get fully rat-arsed. Alan still wasn't in when I tried his place again. I walked back to Newington and it poured.

I was in bed before I finally cried. When I did, it lasted for a long time. I didn't howl, I just lay there and whimpered occasionally as the tears streamed over my face. At some point I stopped crying and started sleeping. I dreamed that Karen married Ricky, and Kerry knocked Cetera out in the fourth round.

Six

Next morning I woke up ill. My head and my stomach were having a competition to see which could hurt the most. It was dead even for about twenty minutes, then my stomach took such a strong lead that my head gave up.

I lay holding myself in a sort of fetal position and looked at the clock on the wall. Seven twenty-five. The thought of the article I hadn't written didn't ease the pain at all. I promised myself another half-hour's rest and self-pity, then I'd get up. Then the pain became so bad I couldn't bear to lie still.

I got up and, almost doubled over, went to the bog. I had a crap and the pain became a little more bearable. I got dressed, then went out and phoned Ricky. I told him to send a doctor over.

It was gastroenteritis. The quack gave me some painkillers and told me to eat nothing and drink only water and fruit juice for a day or two. Ricky and Norrie came over to see how I was. I asked them to phone Ghengis Perring at the *Clarion* and tell him to ring me in the afternoon. Once they'd gone, I lay in bed with my notebook and wrote a reasonable report of the previous day's jollities.

Perring phoned at noon. 'Billy, my son. How're you feeling?'

'I won't die. Just some bug's got into my gut. I'll be all right in a couple of days.' I read the article to him. He took it down in shorthand, then read it back so I could check it. It was all right.

'Has Mallon told any other paper?' asked Perring.

'No, he won't have. I told him I was going to use it. But I don't know about Tambourini.'

'D'you think he would?'

'Nah. Can't see it. I'd expect him to want to keep it quiet. If you get chinned in sparring, you don't advertise it.'

'It's an exclusive, then.'

'Yeah. Though I'll want to tell *Boxing News* next week,' I said. 'I want Cetera to hear about it.'

'As long as we've got it first. We'll run it tomorrow.'

'Send me a cheque while you're at it. I've got a mortgage to pay.'

'Yeah, don't worry. How're you doing, cashwise?'

'It's wobbly.'

'Don't worry.'

The painkillers'd made me drowsy, and I fell asleep after I'd talked to Perring. The phone woke me at three. I made to get up and answer it, then thought that it might be Karen and lay down again. Then I thought it might be Perring with a query about the article. I went out to the hall and picked up the phone. 'Piers.'

'He-llo.'

I nearly dropped the phone. 'Kerry?'

'Mm-hm.' Her voice was trilling, strange. 'Did you phone me last night?'

'Phone you? No.' *What a pathetic little slug you are, Piers.* 'Why?' *That's it, puzzled innocence.*

'I got back from Glasgow late last night, and my mum said a guy with a Scots accent phoned. I knew it wasn't Alex.'

'Well, it wasn't me.' *Fuck's sake. Love the indignation, Billy.*

She laughed, kindly. 'I said unless it was an emergency. I thought it might've been.'

'How're things?'

'All right. Missing you a bit.'

'What were you doing in Glasgow?'

'I'd a job interview.'

'D'you get it?'

'I don't know yet. I think so. It went well.'

You might have got in touch. Trying to keep my tone light, I said, 'Thanks for letting me know you were up.'

'It was just for the day. I wouldn't have had time to see you. Besides, you already know. I need to think.'

'When're you coming back?'

'I don't know. A few more weeks, if I get the job.' I heard someone call to her. 'Billy, I'll have to go. I'm phoning from work.'

'Okay. Kerry?'

'Uh-huh?'

I love you. 'I'm really missing you.'

'I know.' Her voice was gentle. 'Take care.' She hung up.

I went back to bed, but I couldn't get back to sleep. I just sat and looked out of the window for a while. It was quite a nice day, the first that year. It wasn't very warm, but it was bright and sunny. I imagined what it'd be like in the West End of Glasgow. I could almost see the Byres Road area with its arts and crafts shops and pubs in the sunlight. It'd be nice to sit in O'Henry's, the riverside café-bar, drinking Guinness with Karen or Kerry and watching the muddy river rush past. But I wasn't longing. It was nice to be in Edinburgh. It's nice to be anywhere.

Later that night, I felt well enough to do some work. I sat at my typewriter and sketched the background to my book – some biographical detail about Ricky, some of his earlier fights and a detailed description of the fight that'd earned him the title chance.

Then I made a start on the actual writing of the book. I decided to begin with Tambourini lying unconscious in the gym, then work both backwards and forwards from there.

I surprised myself by writing a near-perfect first chapter

in one sitting. I was just finishing it when the phone rang. I wouldn't have answered it, but the chance of it being Kerry made it irresistible. It was Karen.

'Hi, you,' she said brightly. 'I thought you'd moved. I've hardly stopped phoning you since Sunday.'

'I told you I'd be busy. There's been a lot going on.'

'Are you all right? You don't sound too good.'

'I haven't been too well.' I didn't want to say I still wasn't, or she'd have come straight through to nurse me. 'I'm feeling better now.'

'What was it?'

'Stomach pains. Just a bug in something I ate. I'm fine now.'

'I hope you're not living on takeaways.'

'*Me?*' I feigned amazement and she laughed.

'I got Murdo's poem,' she said. I'd posted her a copy on Monday. 'You're right, it's his masterpiece. Has he appeared yet?'

'No sign of him. Ricky can't believe it. He thought Murdo'd practically move in with him. But he's not complaining.'

'I'm sure he's not. How's he doing?'

I told her the events of the day before. 'I've done an article about it. It'll be in tomorrow's *Clarion*.'

'God. Is the guy all right?'

'I expect so. If he'd collapsed or anything when he got back to Glasgow, we'd have heard about it. And I think the hospital'd have kept him in if they'd thought he might not be okay. But it scared us all shitless. We thought Ricky'd killed him.'

'It's horrible. It's stupid.' I already knew how she felt about boxing. I couldn't argue.

'Anyway, it seems to have done Ricky some good,' I said. 'He doesn't seem so nervous now.'

'Mm. That's something.' She hesitated, then said, 'I'd a bit of a bad turn on Monday.'

Christ. 'What happened?'

'Nothing!' She spoke urgently, defensively. 'I just got really upset! I tried to phone like you said, but there was no answer.'

'But you didn't *do* anything?' It was less a question than a plea.

'No. But I got angry with you for not being in. So I scratched your desk.'

'What?'

'I got scissors and scratched all over the top of your desk. I'm sorry.'

I laughed with relief. 'Don't worry about it. I'll varnish it when I get back home.' *Home.* 'In fact, *you* can bloody varnish it,' I added and she laughed nervously.

'Are you sure you don't mind?'

'You can throw hand grenades at the desk for all I care. Just don't hurt yourself.'

'Okay.' A deep breath. 'D'you think I'll ever be all right?'

I fucking hope so. 'Of course. You know you will.'

'I don't.'

'Well, *I* know you will.'

In a small voice she said, 'D'you still love me?'

'Uh-huh.'

'Honest?'

'Yes. I love you, Karen.'

'Can I come through and see you soon?'

'Yeah. I promise.' I added lamely, 'I was wishing I was home earlier today. It was a really nice day, and I kept thinking how nice it'd be in Glasgow.'

'It hasn't been nice here,' Karen said.

'Oh, well,' I said with forced brightness. 'Just as well I didn't jump on a train.'

'I wish you had,' she said seriously.

'You'll see me soon,' I told her again. 'Look, I'll have to go. I'm knackered. I'm going to bed early.'

'All right. I'll call you again soon.'

'Right. I love you. Take care.'

'I love you,' she said.

'Take care of yourself, right?'

'Right. 'Bye.'

I put the phone down. *It's so cruel and stupid. The people you care about most are the ones you're least able to reach. And you can't live any sort of life without hurting people who've been hurt enough.*

Alan appeared about half an hour later. 'Yeah, it's a bastard,' he said when I told him about my illness. 'I've had it. But you'll be back to normal in a couple of days.'

'That's what the quack said.' I made him some tea. I couldn't have any. 'I came round for you twice last night,' I said.

'I'd to go to London. Didn't get back till three in the morning.'

'What were you doing there?'

'Some guy wants to exhibit my stuff.' To Alan, the people he did business with only ever had one of two names: Some Guy, or, the female of the art dealer species, Some Woman. 'You should've left a note saying you'd been round,' he said.

'I didn't think. I was pretty pissed when I came up the second time. I went to the pub between visits.'

'Who with?'

'On my own. I was in a state.' I told him about it, leaving out the most pathetic bits. 'Then Kerry phoned today.'

'She phoned you? Has she made up her mind?'

'No. Her mother told her a guy with a Scots accent had phoned, and she guessed it was me. So she phoned just to find out what was up, since she'd told me not to phone her.'

'What did you say?'

'I said it wasn't me,' I admitted.

'Mm. I'd have done the same. But I think you should forget it.'

'How come?'

'Come on. Is she likely to be into you if she has to think about it?'

'I don't know. She said she needed to think.'

'Doesn't think very fast, does she? How long's it been? Eight months?'

I didn't answer.

'She's probably enjoying it,' Alan said.

'She's not like that. She said she's missing me.' *A bit.*

SEVEN

I first met Kerry the day after Alan moved to Edinburgh. I'd bought a one-bedroom flat in Glasgow Street, in the West End. Shortly after I'd bought the place, Karen had moved in with me. Shortly after that, her illness started to show itself.

She told me she'd had what her doctor called 'schizophrenic episodes' in the past, but that she'd been fine for two years. What triggered the relapse I don't know. There was no reason for it. It came at a time when her luck seemed to be taking a turn for the better: she'd got rid of the cunt she'd married, and her career was blossoming. In addition to her work for *The Voice*, she'd been commissioned to illustrate a couple of children's books. She liked living in the West End and she loved me, which was quite handy since I loved her.

Then she met up with an old flame of hers called schizophrenia, and they got back together. She thought people on TV were plotting against her, that she was terminally ill, that Alan was planning to kill me, and a few dozen other delusions that aren't at all funny when they're happening to somebody you care for.

Fortunately, it didn't last. There was a five-month period of hell, during which she had to give up work and I came very close to becoming an old man in my twenties. Then things settled a bit. Her doctor had prescribed medication that seemed to keep her illness under control. Neither of us knew at the time that a number of people think that the stuff makes you sicker in the long run. They say that if you're not crazy when you start taking it, you soon will be. But, at the time, we were only too grateful for the relief the drugs seemed to bring her.

Her position at *The Voice* had been filled, and she couldn't get one elsewhere. But she did some freelance work, and went ahead with the book illustrations. She was in London to sign a contract the day after we'd said our goodbyes to Alan at Glasgow's Queen Street Station.

He left for Edinburgh on a stifling Thursday in July. It was hot and heavy without being sunny, and Karen and I didn't have much to say to each other. In the evening it began to rain heavily, and continued for most of the night. We made love twice and I told her I was going to miss Alan and she said she knew. Then I slept, and I expect she did too.

I woke alone. I hadn't heard her get up and leave for London. It was a beautiful day, but I felt a bit flat. I left the office at five and went to O'Henry's, where I'd arranged to meet Ricky Mallon. We sat outside in the leafy shade and I drank Guinness and he drank orange juice and we talked about concussion for a while. Then I went home.

I was sitting at my typewriter when the doorbell rang. The first thing I noticed about the girl on the doorstep was that she was taller than me. The second was that she was beautiful.

I'm not using that word loosely. I could say she was pretty or attractive or a dozen other adjectives, but she wasn't. She was beautiful. She had long, shaggy fair hair that looked dark against her perfect skin. She wore jeans and a long, baggy shirt. I could invent some interesting defect, like freckles or a snub nose, but I'm not going to. She was beautiful.

She smiled at me. 'Hi. Is Karen there?' Her accent was English, but I couldn't tell which part.

'No. She's in London.'

'Oh, yeah. She said she was going.' She motioned towards

the open door of the flat next to mine. 'I moved in yesterday. I asked Karen if she'd help me hang a lamp. I was going to do it last night, but I was too tired. I thought she might be back by now.'

'No, she's staying the night down there. She'll be back tomorrow.' I smiled. 'I'll give you a hand if you like.'

'Great. You must be Billy.'

'It's not compulsory, but yeah.'

She laughed. 'My name's Kerry.'

Her living room was crammed full of boxes, bags and cases. There was a couch and a couple of chairs, but they were strewn around without design. 'I've still got tons to unpack,' she said. 'Last night I was so knackered I just made up the bed and went to it.'

'Have you bought this place?' I asked. It'd been empty ever since I'd moved in next door.

'No, my dad owns it. He's going to let it out, but I'm having it while I'm in Glasgow.'

'Where're you from?'

'Shropshire. I'm at college here.'

'What're you doing?'

'Opthalmic optics. Means I'm going to be an optician. What about you?'

'I'm a journalist. Means I'm a journalist.' She laughed again. It was easy to make her laugh. 'I'm deputy editor of *The Voice*.'

'Oh? I read it sometimes. It's a good magazine.'

'It could be a lot better. But it keeps me in the luxuries I'm used to, like eating and living indoors.'

The lamp she wanted to hang was a huge thing, with hundreds of tiny shells hanging on strings. The strings were all tangled together, and that was where I came in. I'd expected to spend a few minutes helping her hang a lamp in an awkward place; instead, I spent more than an hour untangling the strings. We chatted, and I learned that she was twenty-two and in her final year at Glasgow College of Technology.

When we'd untangled the last strings, she hung the lamp next to the window and switched it on. The shells lit up in a myriad of colours. 'Nice?' she said in this little-girl way she had.

'Uh-huh.' I wasn't looking at the lamp. There in that light, she was lovely enough to give you a lump in the throat and elsewhere.

It was still light outside, but she left the lamp on. She went to the kitchen and came back with two mugs of tea. 'No sugar, you said?'

I nodded. 'Just milk.'

She handed me a mug and sat next to me on the couch. She curled up, drawing her knees up to her chest, and took a mouthful of tea. 'Unpacking's a nightmare,' she sighed.

I laughed. 'Karen'll give you a hand tomorrow. I'd help too, but I'll be working.'

'On a Saturday?'

'Yeah. I've got to interview a gay Buddhist who's making a film about Rolf Harris. But Karen'll help.'

'Karen's nice.'

'I think so.' I looked around the room. She'd still a lot left to unpack. I saw a guitar case lying amongst the boxes and bags. 'You play guitar?'

'Nah. I've just started learning. Do you?'

'Yeah. Badly.'

Kerry looked at the guitar case. 'It got bumped a bit on the journey here.'

'Don't worry, they're durable. They're designed for hippies to lug all over Europe on a railcard.'

'It'll be well out of tune, though,' she said. The hint was unmistakeable.

'I'll have a go if you like. But I'm pretty tone deaf.' I went and got the guitar and sat down again. It was a Fender, and about the most expensive one on the market. I'd already gathered that she wasn't poor.

I plucked each string. It wasn't too badly out of tune. I

fixed the two strings that were out and handed the guitar to her. 'There. That's near enough.'

She handed it back to me. 'Let's hear you play something.'

I played and sang a couple of Woodstock standards. 'You're not that bad,' she said.

'I am. It's amazing what you can do with three chords.' I picked the strings. 'This is one of my favourites.' I sang a dark, lonely ballad of a failed relationship. Kerry hummed along, but smiled a bit sourly when I finished.

'It's good. I should get a copy of the lyrics for my boyfriend. I'll be needing them soon.'

'How come?'

'I don't see it lasting much longer. He treats me like shit.'

'Are you going to chuck him?'

'I don't know. He might chuck me.' As if to change the subject, she said, 'You've got a funny accent. Are you from Glasgow?'

'Yeah.' I put the guitar back in its case. 'The accent's just well-travelled Possil. I've wandered a bit.'

'Where?'

'America and France, just to float around. And I've boxed in Nigeria, Italy and Spain.'

'You did *what* there?' She obviously thought she'd misheard.

'Boxed.' I smiled at her. 'Believe it or not, I used to be a professional boxer.'

She stared at me. I'm so thin, I have to walk around in the shower to get wet. 'Boxing? Like, fighting? In a ring?'

'Uh-huh.' I laughed at her disbelief.

'You don't look like a boxer.'

'I know.'

'What's your surname?'

'Piers.' I looked at her hopefully. 'Heard of me?'

'No, I don't think so. But I don't know much about boxing. I don't like it.'

'I don't blame you.'

'You don't seem a violent sort of person.'

'I'm as violent as anybody else,' I said. 'The reason they can't get rid of boxing is that it's something everybody – or every guy, anyway – wants to be able to do.'

'Mm. I don't know. I can't imagine my dad or my boyfriend doing it.'

'You said you couldn't imagine me doing it, either. Even if they hate it, everybody'd like to be *able* to do it. Even the gentlest guys you know. They can deny it, but everybody'd like to be able to punch a guy on the jaw and watch him fall apart.'

'Why'd you give it up?' she asked.

'I didn't like it.'

'So why'd you start in the first place?'

'I was thirteen. I was in care, and I wanted to be good at something. I was hopeless at schoolwork, and worse than hopeless at sports. But I knew I could fight. There was a boxing club, so I went along.' That was simplistic enough to be a downright lie; I remembered the feeling I'd had in my first fight, the other kid pinned on the ropes, nose bleeding, as I slammed him on the jaw and the referee stopped it in the first round. I added, 'But mainly it was because I wanted to be able to do it.'

'Why were you in care? D'you mind me asking?' said Kerry.

Karen knew and so did Alan. I'd told anybody else who'd ever asked to go and fuck themselves, and there was no reason not to tell Kerry the same. Instead I told her, 'I was abused by my parents. When I was nine, they tried to kill me. Tried to burn me to death.'

Kerry just looked at me. There was no trace of morbid interest, or feigned horrified sympathy.

'They held me in the coal fire. My sister screamed the place down, and some neighbours got the police.'

'Were you burned badly?' Her tone was level.

'It was nothing that two years of skin grafts didn't fix.'

'What about your family?'

'I don't know. I don't want to know.'

If she was shocked, she wasn't showing it. 'D'you know why they did that to you?'

I shook my head. 'I don't know. It took me ages to hate them. I used to think it was my fault because it was me they did it to. But it was them. I was just the one they were going to do it to.'

She nodded. 'Yeah. I think I know what you mean.' And I think she did. I think she knew a lot.

Four hours and about a gallon of tea later, I left. 'You're only the third person I've ever told,' I said as she saw me out.

She grinned at me. 'I don't whine about my boyfriend trouble to everybody, either. You're the *first* person I've talked to about Alex.'

It seemed like we were friends.

EIGHT

'Time! *Time!*' shouted Norrie. I leaned on the ropes, legs weak from exhaustion. Sweat stung my eyes. Norrie looked at me. 'Fuck's *sake*, Billy . . .'

I'd just given us all a shock by boxing three hard rounds with Ricky. What started as a light sparring session'd become more brisk as I caught him with sharp hooks to the head. It got downright brutal as it heated up and we both put combinations of punches together. He wasn't trying to knock me out, but he wasn't playing around either. But I'd hit him as often as he'd hit me, and tied him up whenever he'd got close enough to hurt me with body punches. By the third round I was so tired that I held on to him just to keep from falling down.

'Another round?' Ricky asked me. His face was beaded with sweat. Clouds of steam rose from his body.

I shook my head. 'I couldn't,' I croaked.

'You did well,' he told me.

'He did *great*,' Norrie said, helping me off with the gloves. I knew I had.

Ricky and I showered. It was a fortnight since he'd knocked out Tambourini. Norrie'd hired two lightweights from London to spar with Ricky, but both had fights arranged and it'd be nearly a week before they could come. In the mean-time, I'd spar with Ricky one day, and Chris Moyer'd go in the next. Having seen the punches Moyer had to take, I wasn't surprised he needed a day to recover between sessions.

I could tell that Ricky was worried by the absence of demanding sparmates so close to the fight, but there wasn't much to be done. Scottish boxers are a race of pygmies. There was just nobody in Ricky's league on the Scottish fight scene. Tambourini'd been about the best available. Moyer was tough and willing, but his speciality was just absorbing punishment. He'd no skill, and little hitting power.

It was Norrie's fault. He should have hired at least three top men well in advance, even if he and Ricky had to set up training camp in London to do it. But you couldn't blame him too much. He was one of the best managers in Scotland, but that's like being the sanest person in Broadmoor. He was really just a glorified amateur club coach. But Ricky was better off with him than he'd have been with the big names in London. At least Norrie cared about him. If Norrie got him hurt, it'd be through stupidity, not greed or callousness. Unfortunately, what he lacked in greed and callousness, he more than made up for in stupidity.

After we'd showered, we went upstairs to the flat and watched a video of Cetera's last fight. I wasn't too keen on that. It's a mistake to watch endless film of your opponent fighting somebody else; more often than not, when you get in the ring with him, his style's so different you wonder if it's the same guy.

Watching the video seemed to help Ricky's confidence, though. Cetera was a good fighter, but he was easy to hit. He'd a habit of leaning away from punches, rather than moving out of distance.

'See that?' Norrie said to Ricky, who nodded. 'If he does that, you can catch him. Make him lean back with three or four jabs till he can't lean back any further. Then bang him with a big right over the top.'

Ricky nodded again, but said nothing. 'You can't count too much on that,' I remarked. 'His camp'll have noticed it too. They've probably fixed it by now.' Norrie shot me a look that could've frozen the sun. He liked everything he said about tactics to be taken as the word of God.

The fight we were watching'd taken place nine months before. Cetera was defending his title against Peter Negron, a rugged fighter from Nebraska. Things were pretty even going into the fifth round, then Cetera showed why, in a sport where each weight had about three world champions, he was the only lightweight champion: he let go a single left hook, and a few seconds later the ref was shouting for a doctor.

Ricky didn't seem perturbed. 'I'd have put Negron out of it in the first round,' he said. That was probably true, but I didn't think he should try walking into one of Cetera's left hooks.

I left at around six in the evening. Norrie was cooking steaks for himself and Ricky, and the smell was cloying. As Ricky saw me out, he said, 'Liz phoned this morning. Said she met Karen yesterday.' I hadn't spoken to Karen for over a week. 'Seems she's been trying to phone you, but you're never in.'

'She knows I'm busy. I'll call her soon,' I said. 'How's Liz?'

'All right. Pissed off at not seeing me.'

It was a nice evening, chilly but clear. I went up for Alan and we went for a walk by the Water of Leith in Stockbridge. It reminded me of our walks by the Clyde in Glasgow, but this was much more idyllic.

'I'm having a party in a fortnight's time,' he told me. 'You coming?'

'Yeah. Fine.'

'I take it you won't be bringing Karen. Or is that a stupid question?'

'That's a stupid question.'

'How's your book going?'

'Great,' I said.

'Think you'll get it published?'

'If I can keep writing as well as I'm doing now.'

'Any more calls from Kerry?'

'No,' I said.

When I got back to my bedsit at ten that evening, the phone was ringing. What Ricky'd said about Karen's attempts to contact me made me guilty enough to answer it. It was her. I expected a rant about my never being in, but she sounded relaxed and cheerful.

'Hi! Finally got you!' she said. 'I was starting to forget what your voice sounded like.'

'Yeah. I've been really busy. How've you been?' I asked.

'Not so bad. No more bad turns. But I'm missing you.'

'Missing you.'

'Have you started writing your book?'

'Uh-huh. It's coming along.' A pause, then I said. 'You sound bright.'

'Yeah. That's what I called to tell you. I'm going away for a fortnight. With Morag.'

Maybe there is a God. 'How come? Where to?' I tried to keep the delight out of my voice.

'Brighton. Morag's sister lives there. Morag and her boy-friend were going down for a week, but they've split up. So she's asked me to go instead.'

'Great. It'll do you good.'

'I know. I'm looking forward to it.'

'When're you leaving?'

'Tomorrow. I've been trying to phone you all week to let you know. If I couldn't get hold of you tonight I was going to write and tell you.'

'Mm. I'm sorry you couldn't reach me. I've been really busy, like I said.'

'It's okay. But I'd like to have seen you before I went.'

'Nah, I wouldn't have been able to fit it in.' *I'd an urgent case of not wanting to see you that I just couldn't get out of.*

'Well, let's see each other as soon as I get back. Please.'

'I'll do my best.'

'How's Ricky?'

'Fine. His training's going well. He's confident.'

'D'you think he'll win?'

'I'm almost sure he will. But it's no foregone conclusion. It wouldn't be the first time the condemned man shot the firing squad.'

She laughed. 'You should put that line in your book.'

'I already have.'

'I love you,' she said, then laughed and added, 'Well . . . a little bit.'

'Love you. A *big* bit,' I said, and she laughed again.

'Right. I'm going. Give Ricky my love.'

'I will.'

'And Alan my lust.'

'Uh-huh. Enjoy yourself.'

'Love you.'

'Love you. Piss off. I've got work to do.'

'That's all I wanted. A kind word to keep me going till I get back.' She hadn't been so cheery in nearly a year. 'Bye.'

Three days after Karen left, I got a postcard from her.

Dear Billy,

Brighton's here. Wish you were nice. You wouldn't like it here, it's crawling with Tories. Even the tramps wear I LOVE MAGGIE hats. Very strange. But it's nice. Morag and I went for a drink and got chatted up by some acne with men attached. (We said no.) Missing you. Hope your book's going well. See you soon (I hope).

Love you lots.
Me.

The book *was* going well. I sent two specimen chapters and an outline to my publisher, and I can't say I was surprised when they replied immediately, saying they liked it and looked forward to seeing the rest. I was almost too busy to think about Kerry or feel guilty about Karen. All I did was go to the gym and box with Ricky, or sit at my desk writing and listening to tapes or the radio. In addition to working on my book, I wrote several articles about Ricky for the *Glasgow Clarion* and a couple for national papers. My money was running low, and if it hadn't been for my articles being bought, I might have had to abandon the book and go back to Glasgow.

On the rare occasions when I wasn't working, Ricky and I would play chess or watch TV together. We liked wildlife programmes best. We'd usually end up supporting a particular animal and hoping it didn't get eaten.

I didn't think Kerry'd phone, and she didn't. Karen rang from Brighton once, to let me know when she'd be back. I realised it was a couple of days before Alan's party. I'd hoped she'd still be in Brighton so I'd feel less guilty about not telling her about the party.

Ricky received another poem from Murdo Donald, who still hadn't put in an appearance. This was a four-line classic that we felt sure must herald a visit from the bard himself.

UNCERTAINTIES

by

Murdo Donald

It's an unclear road up life's stepladder.
So Ricky, my son, hold up a candelabra.
Keep on smiling, never be a sobster –
Remember that the world's your lobster.

But Murdo never materialised, and this was the last poem he sent.

NINE

I didn't like the way Ricky's training was going. I don't think Norrie did either, though, knowing it was his fault, he tried to pretend nothing was wrong. The two fighters from London, Cordwell Lynch and Hironomous Dwornitzcech, had arrived, and both had shown themselves to be more than capable sparring partners. But Norrie, panicked at not having got hold of quality sparmates until three weeks before the fight, demanded a ludicrous amount of work from Ricky. He had him spar ten rounds – just two rounds short of the actual world championship distance – a day. Four would have been about right.

Ricky'd start by knocking hell out of Chris Moyer for a couple of rounds, then do a hard three with Dwornitzcech, who was a murderous puncher. Then he'd do another three with the elusive – and dangerous – Lynch. To finish off, he'd box a brisk two rounds with me.

It was ridiculous, and after two days of it I said so to Norrie. He turned on me in a fury. 'What the fuck am I supposed to let him do? He's got *three weeks* to go. He can't spar in the final week, so that gives him just *two fucking weeks* of sparring. What should I do? Tell him to just shadow-box?'

We were alone in the gym. Ricky and the others were showering. I'd waited behind to speak to Norrie. 'And whose fault is that?' I said, doing my best not to yell at him. A screaming match wouldn't get us anywhere.

He just looked at me, then said, 'Listen. You're here as our guest. If you don't like the way we train, fuck off.' He turned and went upstairs.

I didn't fuck off, though I was tempted to. I'd started the book, and I meant to finish it. And I didn't have so many friends I could afford to abandon one because his manager told me to.

I had a shower after the sparmates had left and Ricky'd gone upstairs to the flat. I came out of the changing room to find Norrie waiting in the gym. In a low voice, he apologised for what he'd said, and asked me not to tell Ricky. I said I wouldn't.

Next day, the argument sorted itself out. From the moment Ricky started the work-out, it was obvious that something was wrong. When he skipped, he tripped the rope a few times, and his movements were mechanical and lifeless. But it wasn't till he'd done two rounds on the heavy bag that I realised he'd overtrained.

Nobody – boxers, trainers, doctors, or anybody else – understands what being overtrained actually means. But every experienced boxing man knows its cause and what it does to you. Punish your body too severely in too short a time, and you slip past your peak of fitness and become stale. You suddenly find you've no co-ordination; however hard you work, you hardly sweat or don't sweat at all; you get tired easily, and mentally you're flat and unmotivated. And Ricky was showing all the symptoms.

I didn't mention it, knowing the reaction I'd get from Norrie, who pretended he hadn't noticed anything. Ricky didn't seem worried, just listless and disinterested. He went through the motions of doing some floor exercises, then got gloved up for sparring.

Even Chris Moyer managed to hold his own with him for two rounds. If Ricky'd moved any slower, *rigor mortis* would've set in. Norrie still pretended nothing was wrong, and I just watched and said nothing. I don't know whether Dwornitzcech or Lynch noticed, but Dwornitzcech soon found out.

In the first round of sparring, Dwornitzcech slipped an overhand right and countered with a left hook to the side of the head. Ricky sat down hard.

Dwornitzcech looked at him, shocked. 'You okay? I wasn't trying to – '

Ricky just sat there on the canvas, shaking his head. Norrie looked aghast. 'What the fuck's the matter with you?'

'Don't know,' Ricky mumbled, getting to his feet. There wasn't a drop of sweat on the front of his T-shirt.

Norrie looked at me, then back at Ricky. 'I think I know,' he admitted.

'Fuck's sake.' Alan shook his head. 'And a wanker like that's in charge of the number one contender for the world title?' We were in a pub near his flat. I'd just been telling him about my quarrel with Norrie.

'Uh-huh. Trouble is, he's the best manager in Scotland. You wouldn't believe what some of the others're like.' I drank some Guinness, the first I'd had in a while because of my finances. 'But he's a fucking arsehole. He's getting his man ready for a world title fight, and he treats it like an amateur club match. It's fucking farcical.'

'So what happens now?'

'Well, now the cunt admits Ricky's overtrained. So he's told him to take a few days off, just to do what he likes. That should fix it. But it means eating and drinking what he likes. It won't do much for his fitness, or his weight. He's got to be nine stone nine at the fight. And it's so *soon*.'

'D'you still think he'll win?'

Yeah, probably. But it should have been nearly a certainty.' I finished my pint, and started on the one next to it that Alan had bought me a couple of minutes earlier. I was so riled I was considering getting shitfaced. 'If he can get back to his peak of fitness, I don't think the lack of sparring'll do much harm. He's been sparring most days for the past couple of months, though the guys he's been in with haven't been up to much. But it's so fucking *stupid*. He's started the really tough sparring when he should be easing off.'

'But if this guy decked him with sparring gloves on, what'll the champion do if he catches him with one?' said Alan.

I made a face. 'Don't talk about it. We watched a video of Cetera last week. He can bang. He finished it with one punch.'

'Can he hit as hard as Ricky?'

'I don't think so, but he's more accurate. The fight could come down to who can take the best shot. If it does, I don't know who to pick. Neither've ever been decked. Today was Ricky's first time, but I hope that was just because he's overtrained. That's what it does to you, fucks your punch resistance.'

'How well does Ricky normally take a punch?' Alan asked. 'Has he ever been tested?'

'Oh, yeah. He's got a good chin. You should've seen the punishment he had to take from Wilfredo Santana. He just soaked it up. And Santana could hit as hard as anybody. He killed a sparring partner.'

'What about Cetera? Can he take one?'

'Like I said, he's never been down. He seems sturdy enough. But I've never seen him caught on the chin properly. He's easy to hit, but he's put most of them away too quick.' I was getting drunk. 'No, it's Ricky's fitness I'm worried about. The worst that the crap sparring'll do is leave his timing a bit off, but he'll get over that in no time. Cetera'll be right in front of him, so timing won't be the main thing. But the time off training won't get him any fitter.'

'What's he going to do?' asked Alan.

'Everything you're not supposed to do in training. It's all you can do. You've got to let your body recover.

'Why don't you bring him along to my party?' I'd like to meet him.'

'Mm. I hadn't thought of that. I'll ask him.'

'It'll give you somebody to bring along, if you're not bringing Karen,' said Alan.

He got to meet Ricky before the party. We got a carry-out and went back to my flat that night, but after the first bottle of Guinness I wasn't aware of very much. When I woke in the morning, I was in bed and Alan and Ricky were sitting on the couch drinking mugs of tea. I sat up and looked at them. My mouth tasted as though it might be decomposing.

'Look – it moved!' observed Ricky.

'What time is it?' I croaked.

'Talks as well,' Alan said interestedly. 'Have you been under the affluence of incohol, William m'lad?'

'Oh, go and die.' I lay back down, then decided I felt better sitting up. So I sat up again. 'Can you make some tea?' I asked either or both of them.'

'Right away, Mr Piers. At your command, Mr Piers.' Alan put the kettle on. 'Thy will be done, Mr Piers. Whatever the man says, Mr Piers.'

I looked at Ricky. 'I don't remember you from last night.'

'I wasn't there. I came round about an hour ago. You didn't wake. Alan let me in.'

'What time is it?' I asked again.

'Almost one,' said Alan, handing me a mug of tea. I took a mouthful and felt myself come alive.

'Fuck. I must've been in a stupor.'

'Coma's more like it,' said Alan. 'You didn't even wake when we shaved off your eyebrows.'

'*Shit* – ' I scrambled out of bed to have a look in the mirror. My eyebrows were still there. Alan and Ricky were having convulsions.

'Actually, I wanted to,' said Alan. 'Ricky stopped me.'

'Yeah. I reckoned you were ugly enough,' said Ricky.

It was a gorgeous day. The three of us went to Henderson's in Hanover Street for lunch, then sat on the grass in Princes Street Gardens.

'Has Alan told you about his party?' I asked.

'Yeah, he's invited me. I'm going to ask Liz. I could do with my oats,' he said.

'Why aren't you allowed to fuck during training?' Alan asked him.

'Does your legs in. Takes away your staying power.'

'Yeah, Billy's told me that. But why? What damage does it do?'

Ricky shrugged. 'No idea. Neither has anybody else. It's the same as being overtrained. Nobody knows what's actually *wrong*, just that things aren't right. I mean, a doctor can't examine you and say, "You've no stamina 'cause you were at it like a rabbit last night." But it's real.'

'But you can do it now?' said Alan.

'Yeah. I've overtrained. I'm past being fit. I've got to get over that before I start training again.'

'D'you like boxing?' Alan asked him.

'D'you like having black hair?' asked Ricky, face straight.

Karen phoned me next morning. 'I'm back.'

'Hi, back. You sound like Karen. Have a nice time?'

'Uh-huh. Get my postcard?'

'Yeah, thanks,' I said. 'Any problems while you were down there?'

'No. None at all. I've been feeling great. Hope it lasts.'

'Me too.'

'So,' she said, 'What's this about Alan having a party?'

I should have guessed. 'I take it you've seen Liz?'

'Yes. She says Ricky's asked her to the party.'

'That's right. I was going to call you tonight and ask you.'

'Great. Tomorrow night, is it?'

'Yeah.' We agreed to meet at Edinburgh Waverley Station the following day. Then we said we loved each other. After I'd hung up, I punched the side of the couch and took the name of the Lord in vain.

TEN

Alan's parties were never quiet affairs. In fact, they only just fell short of being orgies. Exotic substances were smoked, much noise was made, the police frequently visited, and a good time was usually had by all. When Karen and I turned into Alan's street, a gentle blend of shouts, screams, laughs, moans, music and breaking glass suggested that this one wasn't going to be different.

'Sounds like somebody's having a party,' Karen said as we reached Alan's close. She looked better than she had since the start of her illness. There was colour in her cheeks and her hair shone. She wore a sombre black outfit that didn't look sombre on her.

'Yeah. Sounds like he's invited half of Edinburgh.' This was Alan's usual method of making sure his parties didn't disturb the neighbours: invite everybody within possible hearing distance.

I had to ring the doorbell for a couple of minutes before he answered it. When he did, he looked at Karen in delighted surprise. 'Karen! I didn't know you were coming!'

That's my buddy, I thought. *Land me in it*. But Karen didn't seem to make anything of what he said.

'I'm not. I always look this happy.' She gave Alan a hug and a kiss. 'Missed you,' she told him.

'Makes two of us. When're you going to dump the ugly

bastard and come and live with me?' he said.

'Don't tempt me.' She kissed him again.

I handed Alan a carrier bag full of cans and bottles. We'd stopped at an off-licence on the way over. 'Thanks,' he said. 'I'll put it in the kitchen with the rest of the stuff.' We followed him into the kitchen, where a girl I didn't know was playing barmaid. 'Billy, Karen, this is Linda,' said Alan, and we swapped hellos. The girl poured Karen a Bacardi and I took a bottle of Guinness. Alan offered me some punch from a massive bucket, but I refused. His punch is famous; it's fruit-flavoured paintstripper.

'Has Ricky arrived?' I asked as we went through to the living room.

'Yeah. Quite a while ago,' said Alan. He pushed open the living room door, and we were greeted with a scene that Salvador Dali'd have approved of.

The room was mobbed. Some people were standing on their heads. Lots were necking. I swear it, some were standing on their heads *and* necking. A girl was dancing with an electric heater. Two guys sat on the floor solemnly combing each other's hair. A girl in a top hat and boiler suit was talking earnestly to a mop. Pink Floyd blasted from the hi-fi.

Ricky and Liz were standing near the window on the other side of the room. As we pushed our way towards them, a girl came up to Alan, and without saying a word, threw her arms around his neck.

'Ah. Hi, Clare. Having a good time?' he said. I'd have thought the fact that she was crying probably meant she wasn't.

'Wantneed talk you to,' the girl informed him. Her eyes were like glittering saucers. I recognised the influence of South America's favourite nasal spray.

'I'll leave you to it,' I told Alan, and did. Karen and I went over to where Ricky was standing with Liz. He was drinking orange juice and she had a glass of punch. She had an arm around him and was kissing his ear and talking into it at the same time.

Ricky saw us first. 'Hi,' he said. 'Didn't think you were going to show up.' He swapped hugs and kisses with Karen, and I did the same with Liz. She was twenty-two, mousey-haired and not bad looking in between outbreaks of acne. She was a medical student; she helped people out of hospital, and Ricky put people in.

'I should've told you,' I said to Ricky. 'I always arrive late for Alan's parties.'

'Don't blame you. It's good now, but it was crap earlier on.'

I wasn't surprised. Alan's parties were always pretty bad before everybody got pissed. Lots of arty English types telling each other they were 'rather wungderful', and women kissing each other as they said hello. Women kissing always remind me of boxers touching gloves before a fight.

'How're you feeling now?' Karen asked Ricky.

'Fine. I've just overtrained a bit. There's nothing wrong with me.'

'Well, watch what you're doing. You don't want to take any chances with this fight.'

'You sound like Billy,' he said.

'Are you really writing a book about Ricky?' Liz asked me.

'Yeah,' I said. 'It's a horror novel.' At that point, a bunch of drunken sculptors came up and started talking to Ricky. Karen and I moved away a bit. I heard one of them ask Liz if she liked Ricky's boxing, and wondered how they knew who he was. I later found out that when they'd arrived at the party, Alan'd turned the music off, called for everybody's attention and announced: 'If anybody gets aggressive when they're pissed, do *not* pick on this guy. He's a boxer. He's the British champion, so it's a *bad* idea.'

Karen and I sat on the floor, our backs against the wall. 'Doesn't look like Ricky's going to have much peace tonight,' I said.

'Poor Liz. She was really looking forward to seeing him.'

'She'll have him to herself tomorrow. If she's sobered up by then.'

Karen laughed. 'I know. She's had a bucket. I should've warned her about that punch.' She put her arm round my neck. 'I'm glad I've got you to myself.' She kissed me on the mouth lightly, then more firmly. She broke the kiss, put her drink down next to her, and kissed me again, hard. The taste of her tongue in my mouth was pleasant, but I wasn't excited. After I'd met her in the station that afternoon, we'd gone round to my bedsit and I'd fucked her, mainly because I was too fed up to think of an excuse not to. She came twice. I didn't think I was going to, and wondered how I'd explain that to her. I tried thinking about Kerry, but it didn't work. After about fifteen minutes (from the bed, I was able to snatch the odd glance at the clock on the wall), I managed to finish. It was an elaborate and not at all satisfying wank.

'All right, break it up.' Alan sat down on the floor next to us.

Karen and I unstuck our faces. 'I thought that girl'd claimed you for the night,' I told Alan.

He took a drink from a can of lager. He still looked fairly sober, but I knew he probably wasn't. 'Who, Clare? Nah, it's nothing like that. She just needed a shoulder to cry on. Her boyfriend got burned today.'

'Christ,' said Karen. 'Was it a bad burn?'

He drank some more lager. 'Pretty bad. They don't mess about at the crematorium.' He looked around the room. 'How're Ricky and Liz doing?'

I was starting to answer when somebody called Alan's name. It was Linda, the girl who'd been taking care of the drinks in the kitchen. She was hurrying across the improvised dance floor, pushing people aside. 'Alan!'

He looked up at her. 'What's up?'

'We've got gatecrashers.'

'Fine. The more the merrier. Have they brought any booze?'

'No, listen. They're just kids. Casuals. They'll cause trouble.'

Just then they came into the room, and I realised she was right.

Edinburgh is a far more violent city than the much-feared Glasgow, and it's due to the legion of football casuals there. From our position on the other side of the room, I counted five of them. They were aged about eighteen or nineteen, and drunk. They all had cans of lager, having helped themselves to the drinks stock in the kitchen. They stood near the door, making almost as much noise as the hi-fi. Nobody paid them any notice and they didn't seem to like it.

I looked at Alan. 'Better get rid of them before they start any bother,' I said. He nodded. I took off my glasses and handed them to Karen.

Alan and I shoved our way over to where the casuals were. They stopped talking as we reached them. I shoved one of them and pointed to the can of lager in his hand. 'Finish that and get the fuck out,' I said. He started to ask who I thought I was pushing. I gave him another push to let him know. 'Shut it. You've got ten minutes to finish those drinks and go. If anybody's here in ten minutes, I'll split his face four different ways.'

They just looked at me and didn't say anything. Neither did Alan, who – in spite of his intimidating bulk – is the most docile guy I've ever known. I turned and walked away, and Alan followed me.

Karen was standing talking to Ricky and Liz. Ricky looked at me as I joined them. 'What's this?'

'It's okay. I don't think there'll be any bother. They're just stupid kids. I gave them ten minutes to leave.'

'D'you think they will?' Karen asked. Liz looked worried.

'I think so. I think Alan's size put a scare into them.'

I was wrong. After ten minutes of our ignoring them so they could leave without losing face, they were still there. They seemed to have got fresh drinks and were getting rowdier.

Alan looked at me. 'We'd better go and speak to them,' he said reluctantly.

'Why don't we just call the police?' said Liz.

'Don't have a phone.'

As we started across the room, Ricky handed his drink to Liz and started after us. 'Just look evil,' I told him. 'If it comes to a fight, get out of the way. You don't want to take any chances.'

'Right,' he said, but I knew he was only saying it.

The casuals saw us coming. 'I told you cunts to get out. Are you going?' I asked them. Ricky stood and glowered at them. Alan stood and looked massive.

The one I'd shoved earlier said, 'We're no' daen' any hairm. We're huvin' a party.' He smirked at me and the others laughed. I realised one of them was female. She should've had her hormones checked.

The people dancing near us realised something was wrong. The dancing stopped, and a second later somebody shut off the music.

'Get out,' I said.

'You're spoiling people's night,' Alan told them lamely.

'We're no' spoilin' anybody's night,' the spokesman said.

'Get out or I'll spoil yours,' I said.

'Fuck off.'

I slapped him hard with my right hand, following it with a shove that put him down. I heard one of them roar 'Ya cunt!' Then there was a humming in my ears and I felt the carpet pressing into my face. Above the humming, I could hear people screaming.

My head felt wet, and when I raised my face from the floor I realised there was blood pouring over it. Alan, white faced, was punching and kicking a couple of the casuals. Ricky, like a wolf amongst sheep, was seeing to three more. All around, guests were shouting and screaming. It was like the room was screaming.

I couldn't feel much in my legs, but I could stand on them all right. Ricky had one of the casuals against a wall and was caving in his ribs with body punches. One of the others was behind Ricky, trying to drag him off. I hit him in the liver, spun him round and kneed him in the balls as hard as I could. He screamed with what I sincerely hope was agony until Ricky turned and split his ear with a left hook. He fell to his knees and just whimpered. I was trying to go and give Alan a hand when I blacked out.

Next thing, I was in the bedroom, lying on Alan's bed. Karen and Liz were with me. Something was wrapped around my head. I tried to touch it, but Karen pulled my hand away. 'Leave it alone. It's a towel. It's to stop the blood.'

'What happened?'

'One of them hit you with a hammer. It was under his jacket. Your scalp's cut.'

For some reason I sniggered. 'Am I okay?'

'You're fine,' said Liz. 'But you'll have to have stitches.'

'I feel brain dead,' I said to Karen, who looked scared.

It worked. She smiled and said, 'You always were.'

'Is Ricky all right?' I asked.

Liz nodded. 'Don't worry about him.'

'Are his hands all right?'

'He says they are.'

'Where is he?'

Karen answered. 'In the kitchen with Alan. They're keeping those kids in there. Somebody's gone out to get the police.'

I sat up in the bed. Karen said 'Billy!' and Liz pushed me back down, telling me to stay where I was. For the first time, I could imagine her as a bossy doctor. In spite of the amount she'd had to drink, she now seemed cold sober.

'I need to go to the bog,' I said.

'All right. Go on,' said Liz.

I sat up again. The towel fell from my head and flopped around my neck. 'At least the bleeding's stopped,' said Karen. Liz nodded. I looked down and saw that I'd bled over Alan's blue duvet cover. I got my legs over the edge of the bed and stood up slowly. The room spun a little, then stayed still.

'Give me a hand,' I said, but Karen had already come to me and put her arm around my waist. They both helped me walk on wobbly legs to the bathroom. Liz waited outside and Karen stayed with me while I had a piss. I was surprised that I had no headache.

I took a look in the mirror above the sink. A cut's always frightening when you can't see it. This one didn't look as bad as it might have after a swipe with a hammer. My hair was crusted with dry or drying blood, and there were dry blood drips on my face.

'Does your head hurt?' asked Karen.

'No,' I said, shaking it to demonstrate. I turned on the tap and splashed some cold water on my face. I'd have liked some on my head, but I didn't want to start the bleeding again.

I could now walk without help. Karen and Liz told me to go back to the bedroom and lie down. I headed for the kitchen and they followed me. The living-room door was open as I passed it, and some people were making a brave attempt to get the party going again. Somebody had put on Bowie's *Starman*, though I couldn't see anybody actually dancing to it.

In the kitchen, Ricky was sitting at the table along with four of our playmates. The other one was lying curled up on the floor, still holding his ribs, or what was left of them. Alan, face like chalk and looking more furious than I'd ever seen him, was sitting at the table, holding an empty wine bottle in his hand. I didn't imagine he was planning to offer anyone a drink.

They all looked round as I went into the kitchen with Karen and Liz at my back. 'Are you all right?' asked Ricky, his face expressionless which meant he was dangerous.

'You shouldn't be out of bed,' Alan said.

'That's what we've told him,' said Liz.

'I'm all right. Have the police been called?'

Alan nodded. 'I sent Linda out to phone about ten minutes ago.'

I looked at Ricky. 'You'd better get out of here, then. It'd look great if the papers heard you were part of this.'

'Liz and I were going to run you to the hospital,' he said.

'I'll do it,' Alan told him. 'Billy's right. I hadn't thought of it.' He glared at the casuals. 'I'll be okay with them.' He waved the wine bottle in the air. 'If anybody wants to try leaving they can have this in the face.'

Ricky really didn't want to leave, but Liz and Alan made him see sense. As they left, Liz said they'd call me tomorrow and arrange to meet Karen and me, if I felt up to it.

After they'd gone, I asked Karen to get me a drink. The drink stock had been moved to the living room. 'Liz said not to let you have any. You shouldn't drink when you've had a concussion.'

'Just lemonade, then. I'm parched.' When she'd gone to find some, I looked at the casuals. 'Who was it that hit me?' Nobody answered. I looked at Alan. 'Which one?'

'Him.' He pointed with the bottle.

'Was it you?' I smiled benignly at the one he'd picked.

He was pimply, with streaked hair. 'Get tae fuck,' he said without looking at me.

I briefly thought of getting the hammer and giving him one back, but I didn't. Instead I took the towel that still hung round my neck, wrapped it round my right fist, and hit him in the mouth with a power I didn't know I still had. It took out all of his upper front teeth and a few of the lower ones.

None of his friends said anything. Neither did Alan. 'Anybody else want some?' I asked, and one of them started to cry. It wasn't the girl.

It was a while before I got to hospital. The pigs arrived and started taking statements from everybody. They took a while getting round to me, and when they did, something pretty embarrassing happened: I was sick. It happened so suddenly that I didn't make it to the toilet just in time, and brought up a little on to Alan's hall carpet. Then I was on my knees in front of the toilet bowl, and Alan was taking off my shirt as I puked.

After taking our – edited – statements, the pigs wanted to speak to some of the other guests. Alan felt he ought to stay around, so he gave Karen his car keys and she drove me to the City Hospital. They cleaned up my scalp, put in a few stitches and told me to find party games that weren't so rough.

Karen drove me to my bedsit in Newington. I was so exhausted I could hardly climb the stairs. My face and body felt sticky. My throat hurt and my mouth still tasted of vomit. When we got into my room I lay on the bed and let Karen undress me as if I was two years old. She turned back the quilt for me, and I got under it. I closed my eyes and she sat on the edge of the bed and stroked my hair.

'Are you all right?' she finally said.

'Uh-huh.' Tired as I was, I wasn't at all sleepy.

'I really got a scare tonight.'

'Me too.' I didn't open my eyes.

I heard her undress, then she got into bed next to me. She hugged me tight and said, 'Are you sore?'

'No.' Her naked warmth was nice. 'No pain at all. Just tired.'

She kissed me. 'Good.' She kissed me again. We lay on our sides, holding each other as I half-heartedly returned her kisses. Then without warning, she pushed me on to my back, went down on me and sucked me gently until I came. This time I didn't have to try. I was thinking of our first time together. That was in a dingy bedsit too.

She told me she loved me. I pretended to be asleep and didn't answer. She said it again in a whisper, and I heard myself say, 'Love you.'

I felt as tired as I ever had, but I couldn't sleep. I lay awake for a long time and looked at the patterns the streetlamps made on the ceiling. Karen slept snuggled against me. Her stomach was pressed to my side and we were both sweating a little.

I thought about Kerry. Masochistically, I imagined her with Alex. I pictured them in her bedroom in Glasgow as he undressed her. I knew he always undressed her because she'd told me. I tried to stop thinking about it and managed to. Instead I thought of how good it'd be if it were her I had to share things with. I imagined us living together in Glasgow, or even just living next door to each other as we did. I imagined us coming home from somewhere, maybe a party or something. We'd make tea and talk and laugh as we drank it, then we'd go through to the bedroom and we'd start to kiss and I'd undress her, or she might undress herself. Then we'd make love and it'd be great and we'd lie holding each other all night and we might sweat a little but it'd be nice and we'd both be happy where we were. In the morning we'd wake still holding each other and we'd smile and maybe make love again and we'd be happy and I'd never hurt her.

ELEVEN

The doctor at the hospital had said I'd have a hell of a headache next morning, but he was wrong. I woke at noon feeling fine. Sunlight was streaming through the big windows, and Karen was sitting on the couch reading a paper.

She looked at me and smiled as I sat up in bed. 'Morning. How're you feeling?'

'Great.'

'There's a note from Alan,' she told me. 'He came round to get his car, but you didn't wake.' She came over to the bed.

'You should've wakened me.' I took the note from her.

'Alan said not to, and I didn't want to anyway. Better to let you sleep off last night. D'you want some tea?'

'Yeah, please.' I lay back and read the note.

Dear Billy,

    Came round for the car, but you were still asleep.

    Well, I hope you're thoroughly ashamed of yourself. I was appalled at what you did to that poor, innocent, misguided little lamb. The sight of one of God's children bleeding, with eyes pleading for a fatherly ear to tell his troubles to . . . it just filled me with the humanitarian urge to smash a bottle over his head.

    Anyway, hope you're feeling okay. Karen says the hospital

don't think your brain's damaged any worse than it was already, which'd be difficult. I'll phone you tonight or tomorrow to see if you're dead.

Well, must run along. I've still got some gerbils left to sellotape to the ceiling.

Kill a socialist for Jesus.

Alan

Karen handed me a cup of tea. 'Haven't you got anything to eat in this place?' she asked.

I took a mouthful, shaking my head. 'Just some bread in my cupboard in the kitchen.'

'I bloody knew it!' She ruffled my hair gently. 'You've been living on takeaways.'

'Mostly, yeah. I've eaten at Alan's or Ricky's a few times, too. I've been too busy to cook for myself.'

'Too lazy, you mean. I'll nip out and get us some breakfast. What d'you want?'

'Nah, don't bother. Wait till I drink my tea and we'll go to a café and get something. It seems quite a nice day.'

'It is. It's lovely. I went out earlier on to get a paper.'

'Let's see it,' I said, and she passed over a copy of the *The Scotsman*. I glanced at the front-page headlines. A survey had shown that the majority of Scots felt that the English Tory Government was ruining Scotland. Surprise, surprise. I turned to the sports pages and found an article about the fight, along with a photo of Michael Cetera.

I read it as I finished my tea. There wasn't much to it. It just said that Cetera's training was going well, and that his chief sparring partner was Stevie Ramirez, the guy Ricky'd hammered in two rounds to earn the world title chance. Neither fact meant anything, except that Cetera was being prepared the way a pro fighter should be, and Ricky wasn't.

Karen had read the article too. 'I see Stevie Ramirez is sparring with Cetera,' she said as I put down my mug and stretched.

'Uh-huh. Only means he's getting good sparring. Ramirez can't teach him anything about Ricky.' I folded the paper and started to get out of bed. 'He can tell him what it's like having him knock the shit out of you, but that's all.'

'It was a terrible beating.'

'It certainly was.' I got up, started to walk, and nearly fell over. '*Shit!*'

Karen grabbed my arm. 'What's wrong?'

'It's all right. My knee's a bit stiff, that's all. I must've hurt it when I fell last night.' I limped about the room. It wasn't too bad, more stiff than sore. I knew it'd wear off once I'd used it a little.

I looked in the mirror. My head was lumpy, but I wasn't too bad. I was getting dressed when the phone rang. Karen went to answer it, and came back about a minute later. 'It's Ricky,' she said. I went out to the hall and picked up the phone.

'Hi, you all right?' asked Ricky. He sounded pretty bright. I was willing to bet that Liz was, too.

I carried the phone through to my room. 'Yeah, I'm fine. My knee hurts a bit, though.'

'You must've fallen on it when that cunt decked you last night.'

'Yeah.'

'Listen, the reason I'm calling – d'you and Karen fancy coming to the beach or something for the day? I've got Norrie's car.'

I looked at Karen. 'Hang on and I'll ask herself,' I told Ricky, but Karen was already nodding at me.

'I asked her,' Ricky said. 'She said she fancied going if you felt up to it.'

'Yeah, okay then.'

'Have you got your guitar in Edinburgh with you?'

'Uh-huh.'

'Bring it along, then. What time'll we pick you up?'

'Soon as you like, as long as we can go and get something to eat first. I'm just up. We haven't had breakfast yet.'

'We've been up since seven. Right, we'll be over there in about half an hour.'

And they were. Just after one o'clock, Ricky and Liz arrived in Norrie's car, minus Norrie. It was a cloudless, blistering hot day. I slung my guitar and a couple of jumpers in the boot of the car, and we drove to Henderson's and had lunch. Karen, Liz and I also had a couple of glasses of wine, while Ricky stuck to grape juice. Then we drove to a delicatessen and stocked the car boot with food, three bottles of wine and four cartons of fruit juice. Then we headed for the beach twenty minutes from the city.

I sat in the front passenger seat, Karen and Liz in the back as Ricky drove. Like the rest of us, he was wearing jeans and a T-shirt, and his muscles made him look more like a statue than a human being. His squat bulk seemed to fill the driver's seat.

'There's a bit in *The Scotsman* about Cetera,' I told him.

'Yeah. I saw it. He's taking lessons in getting battered from Stevie Ramirez.'

I laughed. 'That's more or less what I was saying to Karen.' We said no more about boxing. Karen didn't like it, and we both knew Liz hated it.

Musselburgh beach was filthy. Most Scottish beaches are nowadays. But, in the sunshine, you could imagine how the beach had been. There were a fair number of people about, and a few were even swimming in the polluted – probably radioactive – sea.

Ricky got a blanket from the car boot and spread it on the sand. Then we unloaded the food and my guitar. We all ate and Ricky drank the fruit juice and the rest of us drank the wine and we sat in the sun and sang just about every Beatles and Dylan song we knew. The harmonies weren't bad. Then we got hoarse and my fingers got sore from playing and we just lay there and talked and then dozed for a while.

Around six, the temperature dropped a little. I got the two jumpers out of the boot, put one on and gave the other to

Karen. Liz got a jacket out of the car. Ricky said he didn't feel cold. The beach was now empty.

We drove back to Edinburgh. Liz wanted to see a film, but nobody else did. We bought a paper and checked the cinema listings anyway, but there was nothing showing that any of us fancied. Instead, we went to a pub in the Royal Mile. I forget its name. It was in a cellar, and we sat at a table near the open fire. My head was starting to hurt, and I wasn't sure if it was the effect of being hit with a hammer, or just drinking too much wine in too much heat. But after a few pints I was feeling no pain. I looked at Ricky and thought that this wasn't the way to prepare for a title fight, but it didn't seem to matter very much.

I like to remember that day, and the evening in particular, yet there was really nothing special about it. We just sat around and talked. Our faces were red and peeling from the sun, and we laughed a lot. Karen and Liz looked great. I felt good and I think everybody else did, too.

Later, when the pub closed, Ricky dropped us off at my bedsit. Liz was going back to Glasgow the next day, and we were all being maudlin. Karen and I gave Liz huge hugs, then not to be left out, Ricky hugged all three of us.

When we got to bed, Karen and I began to kiss and touch each other, but we were too tired to do much and we fell asleep in each other's arms.

TWELVE

I don't know exactly when I fell in love with Kerry. It doesn't matter. I know I loved her.

I saw a lot of her after she moved in next door to me. At first, we'd just bump into each other on the landing or in the street or the local shops. One would ask the other in for a cup of tea, one cup would lead to a dozen, and we'd sit and talk most of the night. Karen didn't mind. I told her I didn't fancy Kerry, which was true when I said it. And she knew about Alex, Kerry's boyfriend.

One night, a few weeks after Kerry'd moved in, I went to see her. Karen was out somewhere with Morag. I'd expected Kerry to be studying, as she usually was in the evenings, but the door was opened by a guy of about my age. He was red-faced and angry and obviously on the way out.

He looked at me and said nothing.

'Hi. Is Kerry – ?' I started to ask. Then she appeared in the doorway behind him. She was pale and I could see that she'd just stopped crying.

'Oh. Hi, Billy.' Her voice was low and husky. The guy stopped looking at me and looked past me. 'Alex, this is Billy. From next door.'

He looked at me again briefly. 'Hello.' And looked at Kerry. 'Phone me if you like.'

'I will,' she said as he went down the stairs. She stepped

back and motioned to me. 'Come in.'

On the way to the living room, she started to cry. 'Sorry.' Her voice was tight.

I sat down on the couch and she sat next to me. 'Give me a cuddle,' she said. I did. 'I've just had a fight with Alex.'

I let her go. 'I gathered. What happened?'

She took off her glasses and wiped her eyes, then wiped the glasses and put them back on. 'D'you want some tea?'

'Yeah, I wouldn't mind. Are you all right?'

'Uh-huh.' She went to the kitchen and came back with the tea a few minutes later. She handed me a mug.

'Thanks. So what happened?'

'I've been thinking about coming off the pill. I've been taking it for four years now. I never planned to take it that long. When Alex came tonight, I told him I was thinking of switching to the cap or something. He said, "That's just to get at me, isn't it?"' Her voice shook. 'I know it doesn't sound that bad, but he was rotten to me all night, like that . . .'

'I know what you mean.'

'Can I have another hug?' she almost whispered as she started to cry again. As I held her, she said against my ear, 'I don't want him to finish. I'm frightened.' I didn't say anything. After a moment she said, with what might have been a laugh, 'You're supposed to say don't worry, he won't go.'

'He won't if he's got any sense.'

'He thinks I'm stupid. He says I'm just using him as a crutch to lean on.' Before I could ask what she meant, she started to cry again.

So it went. I got into the habit of telling her how good she was when Alex had been telling her how hopeless she was. I wish there was some story, something dramatic about how I fell in love with her, but there isn't. For a long time she was just someone I could talk to, and who happened to be gorgeous enough for me to fancy if I wasn't already in love with somebody else. Then I was in love with her.

I didn't put her on a pedestal, though. She'd plenty of faults, and I recognised at least some of them. She was the only grown woman I ever knew who could stamp her foot and cry because she couldn't find a taxi, even though she wasn't in a hurry. But I loved her just the same.

She went home to Shropshire for Christmas, and I missed her. Karen went to her parents. They'd invited me as well, but I didn't go. On Christmas Eve I sat up all night, wondering what I was going to do.

I went to bed at nine in the morning and slept until four in the afternoon, then went out to see if there was anywhere open that I could get a pizza. There wasn't.

When she got back in January, we didn't get off to a good start. Ricky Mallon was guest of honour at a charity amateur boxing dinner at the Hospitality Inn, and I was invited along. Knowing how Karen felt about boxing, there was no point in asking her to partner me. I asked Kerry and – to my slight surprise – she agreed.

Ricky brought Liz. The four of us had a good table, close to the ringside. Ricky, and every other guy in the place, was wearing a tuxedo, but I wore a plain blue suit. I won't wear a tux as a point of principle; I want no part of anything that smacks of exclusiveness. The guy on the door didn't like it and there was a bit of a scene, but he realised I wasn't kidding and backed down. Kerry wore a dark skirt and top that set off her blonde hair beautifully. I forget what Liz wore.

I don't like dinner shows much, but this one wasn't bad. The meal was all right. The people there were actually boxing men and not the usual fat bastards taking their business contacts for a night out.

The fights weren't bad either, except for one. They'd put Andy Connon, a dangerous light heavyweight, in against somebody neither Ricky nor I had heard of, and whose name escapes me now. It went as you'd expect. We watched as Connon, face pinched with intensity, stalked a frightened-looking opponent round the ring. It wasn't even a fight. The guy backpedalled and poked out the occasional half-hearted jab as Connon methodically cut off the ring. When he ran out of space, he went to the ropes and cowered there like an animal waiting to be slaughtered. Connon moved in to do it.

'*Stop the fight, ref! Stop it. Stop the fight!*' Ricky and I were on our feet, shouting along with several others. Connon was raining punches on the huddled joke on the ropes. None of them really got through because of the way the guy was bent over. The ref just stood and looked as Connon stepped back and waited. The guy tentatively looked up, and Connon slammed in a left-right combination, one to either side of the jaw. The guy took the force of the fall on his face, bounced a little and rolled under the bottom rope on to the ring apron. He'd have fallen off if I hadn't rushed over and caught him.

Cradling the stricken fighter's head in my arms, I got my fingers into his mouth and removed his gumshield. In the ring, Connon raised his arms in a victory salute. The ref gazed dumbly down at the motionless form in my arms.

'Somebody get the doctor!' I shouted. Nobody moved. They were all too busy applauding Connon. 'This guy's *hurt*!' I almost screamed. 'Will somebody get the *doctor*!' I saw Ricky say something to a steward, who nodded and went to look.

The guy vomited. I turned his head to the side to let it out. Some of it went over my trousers. I was surprised by how hot it was. He mumbled something. 'Don't worry,' I told him. He was spotty, and no older than eighteen. He moaned. 'Don't worry, mate. You're okay. You're brand-new,' I said. 'Just take it easy. Easy.' He moaned again and started to shake. '*Christ!*' I shouted. 'Can nobody find that fucking doctor?'

'I'm here.' A Liberace lookalike had appeared at my side. I turned on him, almost crying with rage and fright.

'Oh, you made it. That's nice. Hope I didn't drag you away from the bar over a little thing like this. Should I have waited till he died?'

The quack ignored me and began an examination of the casualty. Ricky took me by the arm. 'Leave it, Billy.'

I heard later that one side of the guy's body was permanently paralysed. It happens.

Kerry was quiet on the drive home. I guessed she'd been shaken by what happened.

'So what d'you think of Ricky and Liz?' I asked.

'Ricky seems all right. He doesn't say much. Liz is nice.' She waited a while, then said, 'I don't like you sometimes.'

'What?'

'Sometimes you're like a different person. You were tonight. You weren't like you are when you're just with me.'

'When tonight?'

'Not all the time. But when you swore at the doorman like that. And when that guy got knocked out.'

'The guy was hurt and the doctor wasn't near him. Was I supposed to be pleased?'

'I'm not saying you were wrong. At least you tried to help. But it's what you were *like*. And the same with the doorman. You were like somebody else.'

I saw her the following night. We sat up and talked until two in the morning. As I was leaving, she hugged me. 'Sorry about what I said last night. I didn't mean to hurt your feelings.'

'It's all right. You didn't,' I lied.

'I didn't mean to. It's just that you're like nobody else I know. Your personality, I mean. You're so aggressive. I just realised tonight, when I don't see you for a few weeks, I've got to get used to you all over again.'

'Oh.'

She kissed me on the cheek. 'You're still my best friend.'

Not long after that, Karen's illness showed itself again, though it wasn't as severe as it would be. Kerry was a help. She never minded my knocking on her door in the middle of the night when I needed someone to talk to. And she was having problems of her own; Alex's treatment of her was getting worse. Unlike Karen's husband, he wasn't violent. Sometimes I wished he'd hit her. I thought that'd be the final straw that'd make her get rid of him. Nowadays, I think she'd have taken it.

She told me about one night when she'd gone round to see him with a speech prepared. She'd told him that she was sick of being used, of his only bothering to see her when he felt like a convenient fuck. She was tired of being stood up without as much as a phone call to say he couldn't make it. And she was sure he wasn't being faithful.

He listened to all this, and didn't deny any of it. 'Well, d'you want to finish, then?' he asked.

She started to cry. 'No.'

In the end, I knew I was going to have to tell her. I wondered if she'd any idea already. One night, we'd both been sitting on the floor in front of her gas fire. As it got late and we both got tired, we stretched out, lying on cushions from the couch. We lay facing each other and talked for a few hours more. We'd both taken off our glasses, and she looked like a drowsy kid. Just before I got up and went to my own flat, I started to stroke her hair. She smiled at me. I wanted to fuck her and I knew she'd quite like me to, and we both knew it wasn't going to happen.

The night before her final exam at college, I did something worthy of a lovesick fourteen-year-old: I wrote her an eleven-page letter and stuck it through her letterbox at one in the morning. I don't remember much of the wording, and don't really want to. It ended: '*I honestly don't know that I could make you any happier than he has, but I promise I'd try.*' Yeuch.

When I rang her doorbell the following night, there was no answer. I still don't know whether she was out, or just not answering the door. The morning after that, there was a note from her in my letterbox. It just asked if I'd come in and see her that afternoon.

She didn't smile when she let me in. She'd been packing.

There were two suitcases, a rucksack and a cardboard box on the living-room floor.

'Moving?' I tried to sound flippant as I sat down on the couch.

She sat down next to me. 'Not for good. I'm going home. I can get a job there.' I knew that, having finished her exams, she had to work for a year in an optician's before she qualified. She hadn't been sure where it'd be.

'Why?' I said.

'For my pre-registered year.'

'I know that. I mean, is it because of my letter? Have you tried to get a job in Glasgow?'

'No. I need to get away for a while.'

'Because of my letter?'

'Yeah.'

'Did you have any idea?' I asked.

'No,' she said. 'None at all.'

'D'you feel . . . anything like that for me?'

'I don't know. If I knew, I wouldn't have to go away.'

'You'll be gone for a year.'

'Maybe not. I'll probably try to find something in Glasgow.'

'You got the job pretty suddenly.'

'I don't even know if I've got it yet. I'm pretty sure, though. I've done summer work with them sometimes. When I'd read your letter yesterday, I phoned and asked them. They said there shouldn't be any problem.'

'When're you going?'

'My dad's picking me up at five today.' It was three.

'Are you staying with your folks?'

'Yeah.'

'I love you.'

'I know.' She smiled a little. 'I do care for you.' She gave me her parents' address and phone number. 'You can get in touch with me there if it's an emergency. But only if it is.'

We sat and looked at each other. She said, 'Will you look after my plant?'

'Uh-huh.' My voice was strange. 'Better than you ever did.' Her busy Lizzie was only half alive.

I headed for the door, plant in hand. 'Right,' I said. 'I'll see you whenever.'

'When you've taken it through, get back here and give me a cuddle,' she called after me.

Karen was out. I put the plant in the living room, next to my desk. Then I went back into Kerry's. She was still sitting on the couch. I sat beside her and she put her arms round me. I clung to her and she rubbed my back as I pressed my face into her shoulder. Her hair smelled of coconut shampoo.

We stayed like that for a few minutes. Neither of us said anything. I didn't want to let her go. I think we'd still be sitting there in each other's arms if she hadn't finally broken free and stood up.

'Come on. I've still got stuff to pack.' She bent over and kissed my forehead.

I stood up. 'All right.' *It hurts.* 'I love you.'

She smiled gorgeously. 'I know you do. You're good to me.'

'Will Alex be coming down to visit you?' I hadn't meant to say it.

'I don't know. I suppose so. If he wants to.' As I left, she called, 'Take care.'

When I was out on the landing, unlocking the door to my flat, she came out and kissed me quickly and firmly on the lips. She smiled at me as she went back into her flat.

That was the end of something.

THIRTEEN

I thought Karen would travel back to Glasgow with Liz, but she didn't. Saying she wanted to be absolutely sure I was all right, she stayed another two days. It was all right. She sat around and read, or made me cups of tea while I was writing. Her illness didn't show itself. When she left, I wasn't sorry, but I wasn't glad either. It didn't make much difference.

My injury made any more sparring with Ricky out of the question. I still went to the gym every day to watch. Ricky's timing wasn't what it should have been, but he was all right. He did just the right amount of everything, and was as fit as I'd ever seen him.

His attitude was right, too. He was aggressive and cheerful, looking forward to the fight. The fact that the SECC had sold all ten thousand tickets for the fight, and that TV was paying well to get it live, didn't do anything to depress him.

I hadn't much to do. I'd written as much of my book as I could. I couldn't write the final two chapters until the fight was over. I had no idea about Karen or going back to Glasgow or anything. Karen phoned me a lot.

When I wasn't hanging around the gym, Alan and I'd get pissed or walk by the Water of Leith. Sometimes Ricky and I'd go up Arthur's Seat, which I never liked. I wrote a lot of copy for the *Glasgow Clarion*. I offered to write a preview of the fight for *Boxing News*, the respected trade paper, but they understandably said no. They reckoned that my being part of Ricky's camp would make it a bit one-sided. The *Clarion* had no such qualms, and I wrote a preview saying that, while Cetera's chances would increase the longer the fight lasted, the most probable outcome would be a victory for Ricky in about five or six rounds.

While I was writing the piece, the phone rang twice. I ignored it. It rang again when I'd finished. I answered it. 'Piers.'

'Hello.' It was Kerry.

'Hi,' I said.

'How're you?'

'Okay.'

'I got that job in Glasgow.'

'Great. When're you coming back?'

'Tuesday,' she said. This was Sunday. 'D'you want to get together?'

'Do you?'

'Mm. I've got some news for you.' She sounded like a child keeping a present hidden as a surprise.

'What is it?'

She laughed. 'Can't you guess?'

'No.' I felt panicky.

'What d'you think?'

'I don't think anything. Tell me.'

'I love you, Billy Piers.'

My eyes started to water. 'Are you kidding?'

'No. I know I need my head examined.' She laughed. 'But I'm stuck with it. I love you.'

'I love *you*,' I said, managing not to cry.

'Mm. Hoped you still might.'

'I do.'

'That's all right, then. Quite handy.' Her tone became more serious. 'What about Karen?'

'I don't know.' I couldn't think about Karen. I couldn't think. My right leg was shaking quite violently. 'I'll have to tell her. Have to finish.'

'It's a shame.'

'Yeah. What about Alex?'

'We've finished,' she said.

'When?'

'A while ago.'

'Oh.'

'I haven't heard from him for weeks. I don't suppose I will again.'

Who chucked who?' I asked.

'Does it matter?'

'When d'you start your job?'

'A fortnight, but I'm coming up on Tuesday. When'll I see you?'

Now! Yesterday! 'Soon. Ricky's fight's on Friday. I'm coming through then.'

'Couldn't I see you before then?'

'You could, but I shouldn't. I'm writing the book from the point of view of a member of the camp. I should sit around here and scratch my balls with the others for the rest of the week. If I didn't, something might happen while I was away.'

'Pig. All right.'

'You could come through to Edinburgh,' I said.

She laughed. 'Nah. I'd forgotten what an awkward pig you are. I might as well start getting used to it.'

'Can you love a pig?'

'I do.'

'Oink.'

She laughed again. 'I'll see you on Friday, then?'

'Yeah.'

'What about Karen? Will you tell her by then?'

'I don't think so. She's going to need looking after. This'll fuck her up.'

'You're going to tell her, aren't you?'

'Of course. But I'm not going to phone her up and say it's over. I'll tell her soon. When I'm back in Glasgow.'

'So, where'll I see you? It can't be my place, with her next door.'

'I'll think of something,' I said. 'Call me tomorrow.'

That night, I went round to Alan's and we talked a lot. While we were talking, we also drank a lot. Around midnight, we were walking along Princes Street, arms over each other's shoulders, doing the Monkees walk as best you can with only two people. We came to a phone box.

'Wairraminnit,' I told Alan. 'I love Kerry.'

'That's good.' He patted my back. For some reason, the most likely being drunkenness, I started to cry. 'You okay?' asked Alan.

'Yeah.' Still crying, I lurched into the phone box. I got out my address book and, after a few attempts, managed to dial Kerry's Shropshire number. It rang for a while, then a female voice said, 'Hello?'

'Listen! I love you,' I proclaimed.

'That's nice. So does my husband,' said Kerry's mother. 'Hold on.' A moment later Kerry came on the phone.

'Hello, Billy?' She sounded sleepy.

'Uh-huh.' I was still crying, but she didn't seem to notice it. 'I love you, all right?'

She giggled. 'All right. Are you drunk?'

'D'you love me?' I demanded.

'Yes. Same as I did this afternoon.'

'Did I wake you up?' I said, suddenly full of remorse.

'Yes.'

'Sorry. Didn't mean to.'

She laughed. 'It's all right.'

'Go back to bed. I love you.'

'I love you.'

''Night. I love you.'

'Love you. Goodnight.' I was mumbling things about

loving her and suggesting she go back to bed when she did.

I went out of the phone box. It was a beautiful, warm night. 'What're you crying for?' said Alan.

'It's a lovely night.'

I caught a train to Glasgow on Friday morning. I could've gone in the car with Ricky and Norrie, but on that day I reckoned it'd be best to leave them alone for a while. That night, they had the chance to arrive where they'd been heading for nine years.

The journey was all right. It was ten-thirty, so the morning rush was over and the train wasn't crowded. It was a warm, cloudy day. I drank Coke and watched fields go past the window.

Two days earlier, Karen and Kerry'd phoned me within half an hour of each other. Karen was first. She wasn't going to the fight. 'Liz is going to come round here. We'll watch it on TV or go and see a film or something.'

'Yeah, take her to see a film. Don't let her watch the fight. It'd upset her. She got into a state when she saw him fight Ramirez. And this'll be harder.'

'How is he?'

'Great. He's in good nick, and his attitude's perfect. He can't wait to get at Cetera. But he'll be nervous once he's there.'

'I sent him a good luck card.'

'Yeah, he got it. He tried to ring to say thanks, but you were out.'

'D'you know Kerry's back?'

'No. I knew she was coming back, but I didn't know she'd arrived. I expect she'll call me.'

'Uh-huh. She said she was going to. She looks well.'

I'll bet.

Then Kerry rang. 'Hi. I hear you'd a mishap with some football casuals.'

'Yeah. They'd to take time off being casuals to be casualties. Karen told you.'

'Uh-huh. I was talking to her today.'

'I know. She's just off the blower.'

'She's looking nice.'

'She said the same about you.'

'I've got something for Friday.'

'What?'

'We can stay at Susan's. She's at her mum's for the summer. I've just phoned her. She said I could have the place.' Susan was a friend of hers from college.

'Have you got keys?'

'She'll post them to me first thing tomorrow.'

'Okay.' I thought of Karen and what a shit I used to think Alex was. 'What's the address?'

She told me, and I wrote it down. It was in Cowcaddens, near the Glasgow Tech. 'What time'll you be there?' she asked.

'I don't know. Depends on how long the fight lasts, and how long I hang around after it. But I'll get there.'

'All right. If it's really late, I might fall asleep. Just keep ringing the bell till you get an answer.' She paused, then asked, 'What'll you tell Karen?'

'Leave that to me.' *Ask Alex. He's the expert at being a cunt.*

FOURTEEN

The weigh-in at the SECC wasn't till noon. That gave me just over an hour to spare when I got off the train at Glasgow Queen Street Station. I took the underground over to the West End, getting off at Hillhead. My flat in Glasgow Street was quite close by, but I didn't go there. I'd had no breakfast, so I went to a coffee shop off Byres Road and had tea and a croissant. As I ate, I read the *Glasgow Herald*, which predicted that Ricky'd win inside the distance.

I was walking along Argyle Street on my way to the SECC when a familiar figure walked past me without a word. 'Murdo!' I called and he turned and looked at me.

It was Murdo Donald as I'd never known him before. Usually he was impossible to get away from when you met him. This time, he just looked at me blankly and said, 'Hello, Billy.'

'How're you doing? Ricky got your poems. We thought we'd be seeing you at the gym.'

'No. I haven't been too good.' He looked pretty shabby. His clothes, though always in disgusting taste, were normally new and expensive. 'I'm not bothering much with boxing.'

'How come? What's up?'

'I'm just out of hospital. Depression. I'm getting treatment for it.'

We looked at each other helplessly. I didn't know what to

say, and he probably didn't want to say anything. Finally I said, 'Look, Murdo, I've got to get going. The weigh-in's in twenty minutes. D'you fancy coming?'

He shook his head. 'I told you, I'm not bothering with it. Anyway, I'm meeting my sister.'

'Okay. You've got my phone number, haven't you?' He nodded. 'Right. Give me a ring and come over for a cup of tea, okay?'

He nodded, but I knew he wouldn't. He walked off without saying anything else.

I decided not to tell Ricky about Murdo till after the fight. The weigh-in was in progress when I got to the SECC. Watched by about fifty people, some of them journalists, Ricky was getting on the scales. He looked like an advert for health foods. Norrie was standing next to him, and someone from Cetera's camp was looking on.

The announcement came. 'Mallon weighs 134 pounds.' He was comfortably inside the weight limit. As he stepped off the scale, he caught my eye and beckoned to me. I pushed my way through the onlookers and joined him as he moved away from the scale and put on his dressing gown.

Norrie stayed at the scale as Cetera got on. The champion's face showed no concern as he slipped off his white towelling gown. He was a couple of inches taller than Ricky. He wasn't heavily muscled, but looked tight and strong.

'He looks fit,' said Ricky.

'So do you,' I said.

'Cetera weighs 134¼ pounds,' declared the MC. Cetera got off the scale and put his gown back on. Norrie came over and said hello to me.

A few reporters asked Ricky how he felt. 'Fine,' he said. Was he going to win? 'No, I've come to be beaten.' Everybody laughed. Would he knock Cetera out? 'Go and ask him.' He did it just right. You have to show an abrasive arrogance on the surface, and keep an inner calm.

The press went to speak to Cetera, and we slipped off

to Ricky's changing room. 'How're you feeling, really?'
I asked as he got dressed. Norrie'd gone out to make a
phone call.

'Nervous.' He looked it. 'I didn't sleep much.' Neither had
I. 'I'll be okay once I'm in there.'

'He's just as nervous as you.'

'He didn't look nervous.'

'Neither did you,' I said.

Norrie came in. 'Most of the reporters've fucked off. Let's
get going.' He was right. Only two journalists, both of whom
I knew, were still there. They were in the foyer, talking to
Cetera and his handlers. One of them said hello to me as we
passed them.

Ricky nodded to Cetera, who called, 'God bless you,
Richard,' and I remembered reading somewhere that he was
a born-again Christian. I wondered what his prayers were
like – *Lord, give us this day our daily bread, and please let
me knock fuck out of Mallon tonight.*

Norrie's car was parked across the road from the Kelvin
Hall. As we got in, he asked Ricky, 'Where d'you want to
go for lunch?'

Ricky shook his head. 'I'm not bothered. I don't feel like
eating. I'm not hungry.'

'You'll have to eat something,' Norrie told him.

'I don't think I could,' said Ricky.

'It's just nerves,' said Norrie. 'Once you start to eat, you'll
feel hungry.'

I knew from experience that he was wrong. 'He's right,' I
said. 'You've got to have something.'

'How about a baked potato?' Norrie suggested.

'Mm. Okay. Where?'

'Wherever you like.'

He chose O'Henry's. As we drove, Ricky said he'd read
that Jack Dempsey didn't eat for days before some of his
early fights. 'Not through choice,' I said. 'He was a hobo.
He was fighting so he *could* eat.'

There weren't many people in O'Henry's when we got there.

'Nothing about boxing from now on,' Ricky said as we sat down. Then he smiled and added, 'Please.'

Lunch went okay. Ricky played with his food, but we finally bullied him into finishing it. He didn't say much while Norrie and I awkwardly pretended he wasn't fighting for the world title that evening. When we'd finished eating, I had a glass of orange juice then stood up. 'I'll leave you to it.'

'Okay,' said Norrie. Ricky nodded but didn't say anything. I knew they wanted to be on their own.

'What're you going to do till tonight?' I asked.

'Go over to my house and take it easy,' said Norrie.

'Liz's going to phone me there,' said Ricky.

'Right. I'll see you tonight. Good luck.'

'Come to the changing room when you arrive,' said Ricky.

I didn't want to go home. I'm not a very good liar, and I didn't want to face Karen. I took the underground to St Enoch's Square in the city centre. I wasn't sure what to do. There were friends I could call on, but I didn't feel like talking to anyone. I went for a walk by the River Clyde, but turned back when it started to rain. I thought of going to the Glasgow Film Theatre, but I'd have had to leave before the end of the film. I bought a book in Hatchards, then went to a café in Princes Square. I sat there for the rest of the afternoon, reading and drinking overpriced tea.

I was scared.

The SECC was filled beyond its seating capacity. The promoters'd bent the rules a bit by selling cut-price tickets to people who didn't mind standing. Even that didn't satisfy the demand.

I was on the guest list. The show had started when I arrived, but there was a long while to go before the main event. I went to the bog before going to the arena. There was a dark, wiry man standing at the urinal next to mine. He wore jeans and a T-shirt, and looked familiar. As he finished his piss and started to move away, he looked at me and said, 'Hi, man. How're you doing?' in an American accent.

It was Stevie Ramirez, Ricky's most recent victim. I'd gone to his corner and spoken to him after Ricky'd stopped him in two rounds.

'Oh, hi.' I smiled at him. 'Hear you've been sparring with Cetera.'

'Yeah. I was meant to be fighting tonight as well, but I wrenched my knee.'

'What d'you think'll happen?' I asked as he washed his hands.

'Nothing in it, man. Mallon's too strong. He'll walk right through Mike.' He dried his hands. 'See you later.' He went out, and I took his place at the washbasin.

No booze was allowed into the arena, but most of the fans'd had plenty before they got there. A number had pissed in the aisle. Typical Glasgow – you can't take them anywhere.

My seat was at ringside. Some drongo was sitting on it, and I had to get a steward to move him. A few journalists came over and said hello, but I wasn't in the mood to chat. I sat in silence, drinking Coke and watching a Scots fighter get his face decorated by an American. I hoped it wasn't an omen.

I stirred myself to go and see Ricky. A steward showed me to the dressing room. I knocked, and Norrie called, 'Who is it?'

'Billy.' The door was opened by Charlie Robb, a veteran trainer Norrie'd hired as assistant second. I went in, and Norrie told the steward to let no more visitors in.

It was a small, dingy room. There was a patched leather couch, a few wooden chairs and a rubbing table. Ricky was sitting on the couch next to Norrie. He wore a red tracksuit and old slippers. His hands were taped and bandaged. His face was grim. Charlie Robb sat on one of the chairs, talking to Tam Aitchison, an experienced 'cut man' who'd been enlisted to look after Ricky if he got cut for the first time in his career.

'Hi, Billy.' Norrie smiled at me. Ricky just nodded. Norrie had some envelopes and cards on his lap. 'I'm just opening some good-luck cards. There's one from your mate Alan.' Alan hadn't been able to make it to the fight. He was in London.

'All right?' I asked Ricky. He nodded. 'Did Liz phone you?'

He licked his lips before he spoke. 'Yeah. She's worried. She's going to the pictures with Karen.' He paused. 'I'd've liked her here.'

'It'd only upset her more. Karen'll look after her.'

'Yeah.' He looked at Norrie. 'Let's see the cards.'

'Right. Hold on.' Norrie checked all the cards before finally handing them to Ricky. Sometimes you get abusive letters or even death threats in your mail before such a fight. There were none this time.

It got later. Ricky took off his tracksuit and lay naked on the rubbing table. Aitchison smeared vaseline over his face. There was about half an hour to go. The steward knocked on the door and called, 'The ref's here to see Ricky.' Norrie had insisted that the referee's final instructions to the fighters be given in the dressing rooms rather than in the ring, which is how it's usually done. He planned to have Ricky warm up in the dressing room, go into the ring loose and sweating, and go straight to war at the first bell. There must be no lengthy preliminaries during which he'd get cold. Norrie had also demanded that the American MC, Nathan Di Mambro, keep the introductions short. Any hanging about, he'd warned, and he'd take Ricky right back to the dressing rooms.

'Tell him to wait a minute,' Norrie called to the steward. He looked at me. 'Better let us get on with it, Billy.' He held out his hand and I shook it.

Ricky was lying with his eyes closed. I looked down at him, not sure what to say. 'All the best.' He nodded without opening his eyes. 'Champion's only a word,' I said. 'He's a man. He pisses and shits the same as you do.'

I went back to the arena. The second-last preliminary fight was on. The loser was from Glasgow. He was beaten on points. Then another Scotsman took a one-sided hammering and was stopped in the third.

The ring was cleared, and stayed that way for ten minutes. People were shouting and chanting and singing and the air was rancid with urine and cigarette smoke. Then someone got into the ring, microphone in hand. It was Di Mambro.

Norrie's warning about lengthy introductions must have got to Di Mambro. He started the announcements before either fighter was in sight, let alone in the ring.

'Let's get ready to rumble, *this – is – it!*' The noise of the crowd drowned him out, and he had to wait a few seconds before going on. 'Twelve three-minute rounds for the undisputed lightweight championship of the world . . .'

Suddenly, the spectators went berserk, and I actually became slightly deaf from the roar. They'd seen both camps bringing their fighters to the ring.

FIFTEEN

Ricky was a throwback to an earlier age, to the days of Harry Greb and Mickey Walker. He'd no frills. He was a fighting man who came only to hurt his opponent. He wore no robe as he came down the aisle to the ring. His only top-cover was a white towel, which he threw off before climbing between the ropes.

Seconds after Ricky and his handlers got into the ring, Cetera climbed in, following the tradition that the challenger has to enter the ring first. I couldn't really hear the spectators now; their noise had caused a singing in my ears that was almost painful.

Ricky's body was sheened with sweat. He wore plain black shorts, and black boots with no socks. He disdained the theatrics of trying to outstare his opponent. As Cetera's seconds removed their man's gold satin robe, Ricky prowled around restlessly, shadow-boxing, staring at the floor.

Di Mambro started talking again. At first I couldn't make out what he was saying.

'. . . Glasgow . . . in the red corner, Ricky Mallon.' He said something after that, but the crowd swept it away with a chant that would last throughout the night.

'*Ma-llon, Ma-llon, Ma-llon* . . .'

'In the *blue* corner,' shouted Di Mambro, 'from Sacramento, USA, the undisputed lightweight champion of the world – Michael Cet*era*!'

'*Ma-llon, Ma-llon, Ma-llon . . .*'

McAree, the ref, called both fighters to the centre of the ring and they touched gloves. Cetera glowered at Ricky, who kept looking at his feet.

'Let's get it on, said the ref. Both men went to their corners.

'*Ma-llon, Ma-llon, Ma-llon . . .*'

Norrie put the gumshield in Ricky's mouth.

'Seconds out, round one.'

Cetera came out cautiously, guard tight. Ricky went straight for him, almost running. The champion backed off as Ricky missed with two wild hooks. Cetera landed a couple of jabs, but they were too high to hurt, bouncing off Ricky's forehead. Ricky moved in, trying to get close and work to the body, but Cetera was well tucked up. A fierce left hook from Ricky was absorbed by the arm that covered Cetera's ribs. Then Ricky brought a crude right over the top. It caught Cetera on the side of the head and he sat down hard.

'*Ea-sy, ea-sy, ea-sy . . .*'

The crowd thought it was going to end there and then, but Cetera wasn't in trouble. He was surprised rather than hurt, and was on his feet before the ref had begun the count. Ricky steamed after him but didn't manage to get through a second time. Cetera stayed calm and kept jabbing till the bell. He walked to his corner and sat on his stool. His trainer said something to him and he nodded.

'*Ma-llon, Ma-llon . . .*'

Norrie was standing in front of Ricky as he sat on his stool. He leaned Ricky's head against his chest and rubbed the back of his neck. As Ricky stood up for the second round, Norrie said something and slapped him on the seat of his shorts.

'*Ma-llon, Ma-llon, Ma-llon, Ma-llon . . .*'

'Seconds out, round two.'

Cetera was under heavy pressure. Ricky went for him and didn't let up. He forced Cetera to stand off and box, a style that didn't suit him. Cetera got in a couple of solid hooks, but they didn't seem to trouble Ricky, who won the round clearly. At the bell, he almost walked to the wrong corner through sheer excitement.

Cetera went down again in the third, and this time he was hurt. Ricky might have had him then if he hadn't been too eager and started to swing wildly. Cetera slipped the swings, grabbed and held on, and was still there when the round ended. He looked white and sick as he went to his corner.

Norrie was almost spitting with rage. As Ricky gargled with tepid water, Norrie held a handful of his hair and roared at him, face livid. The seconds, Robb and Aitchison, were nodding vigorously.

'Seconds out, round four.'

Cetera knew his grip on the title was getting slacker, and he tried hard to pull it back in the fourth round. Gumshield exposed in a snarl, he stood his ground as Ricky rushed him. He got through with some good left hooks to the head. Ricky still won the round, but he didn't dominate it as he had the others.

'Seconds out, round five.'

'Seconds out, round six.'

Both men looked weary, but the pace hadn't eased much. Cetera was bleeding from a cut under his right eye, but he'd been giving some back, and Ricky's face was puffy. The cut wouldn't make much difference. Nobody's going to stop a world title fight because of a cut that doesn't affect your vision.

Cetera steadied Ricky with a left hook to the head. Ricky fought back with a barrage of vicious body punches. Most of them missed, but one went into Cetera's liver, and he dropped to his knees.

'*Ma-llon, Ma-llon, Ma-llon, Ma-llon, Ma-llon, Ma-llon, Ma-llon, Ma-llon . . .*'

Ricky walked to the neutral corner and the ref began to count. Cetera struggled to his feet at eight, but he was gone and the ref would've counted him out if the bell hadn't rung at that point.

In the corner, Ricky was being told in no uncertain manner. Norrie didn't let him sit down. He shouted at Ricky and pointed over at Cetera, whose seconds were working on him furiously.

The crowd began to stamp their feet. '*Ma-llon, Ma-llon, Ma-llon, Ma-llon . . .*'

Norrie took Ricky by the arm and led him out to the centre of the ring. He pointed at Cetera again. Ricky looked. The ref said something. Nobody paid any attention.

'*Ma-llon, Ma-llon, Ma-llon . . .*'

Norrie turned and walked back to the corner, leaving Ricky. There was about ten seconds until the start of the round. Cetera's manager shouted to the ref, who told Ricky to get back to his corner. Ricky backed off a couple of steps, but that was all.

'Seconds out, round seven.'

Cetera went to meet Ricky, crouched over to protect his body. He spent most of the first minute just covering up and clinching. The ref had to caution him twice for holding. After the second caution, he stood off and began to mix it with Ricky. A pair of hooks to the head dropped him again.

I shifted in my seat. My back and armpits were running with sweat, plastering my shirt to me. Stay down, I thought. You're beaten. *Stay down.*

Cetera got up. The ref took a long look at him, then ordered, 'Box on.'

Ricky moved in. He began to pummel the champion exhaustedly.

'*Ma-llon, Ma-llon, Ma-llon . . .*'

Cetera fought back as best he could. Towards the end of the round, he unleashed a blistering combination of punches, finishing with a left hook to the chin.

Ricky wobbled, and held on.

'*Ma-llon, Ma-llon . . .*'

Cetera tried to push him off and follow it up, but he hadn't enough left. The ref made them break, then waved them back to work. Ricky belted Cetera with another left hook just before the bell.

Ricky was more tired than I'd ever seen him, and he'd been hurt. But, before the bell rang for the eighth round, he stood up, looked over at Cetera, and took a deep breath. *This round*, I thought. *Get him now. Finish it.*

'Seconds out, round eight.'

Cetera didn't move from his stool, and his seconds didn't leave the ring. His manager called the ref over and said something to him.

'*Ma-llon, Ma-llon, Ma-llon . . .*'

The ref nodded. He went over to Ricky, took him by the wrist, and raised his arm. Norrie jumped into the ring with Robb and Aitchison, and they lifted Ricky on to their shoulders. My ears hurt from the noise of the crowd. I closed my eyes.

When I opened them, Ricky was over in Cetera's corner, hugging him. Nathan Di Mambro was climbing between the ropes. I closed my eyes again and listened to the announcement.

'. . . the winner, and new undisputed lightweight champion of the world – '

'*Ma-llon, Ma-llon . . .*'

SIXTEEN

The party was at the Hospitality Inn. Ricky'd told Cetera he was welcome to come along, but of course he didn't. His seconds'd taken him over to the Western Infirmary to have his cut seen to. I didn't think he'd have to wait very long. The casualty department wasn't likely to be busy – most of the nutters had been at the SECC or glued to their TV sets. It must've been the quietest Friday night the Glasgow police had seen in years.

The press didn't hassle Ricky. They came along to the party and asked him a few questions. He answered them, and that was the end of it. He invited them to come back to the party after they'd filed their stories, and a few did.

Liz arrived around midnight. She told me that Karen'd taken her to see a film, and they'd got the result from a couple of drunks in the street. 'Karen's not coming along here,' she told me.

'Yeah. I knew she wouldn't.' I'd counted on it. 'Should I ring her?'

'Nah. She said she was going to bed. Said to tell Ricky well done, and to tell you to come in quietly and not be too pissed.'

I laughed. 'Go and see Ricky.' She did.

I had a few drinks and chatted to some people. Norrie and I apologised to each other for the friction there'd been in

Edinburgh, and both claimed to be the one to blame. We said a few sickly things and shook hands.

Ricky was sitting in a corner with Liz somewhere. One of the hotel's receptionists came in and announced that Alan had phoned to congratulate him. He'd seen the fight on TV.

I drank some more and lost sight of Ricky again. I went to look for him at about two in the morning. I found Liz, and she said he was looking for me. Then we both searched the room and found him.

'Just to say goodnight,' I told him. 'I'm off home.'

'Oh, right. Yeah.' He looked as though he was sleepwalking. 'Can I have a word before you go?'

'Yeah. What?' It couldn't be about the fight. We'd agreed to meet the next night and do the postmortem then.

'In private,' he said.

Liz didn't like it, but didn't complain. 'See you later,' she said to me, and went up to the bar.

'What's up?' I asked Ricky, wondering if Liz had asked him to retire.

'Not here. Let's get somewhere quiet.'

The only place we could be alone was one of the cloakrooms upstairs. We went in and I closed the door.

'What's up?' I asked again.

Ricky shook his head. 'I don't feel a fucking thing.'

Like Arthur's Seat.

I used the payphone in the hotel foyer. I thought Kerry'd be asleep, but she answered right away. 'Hello?'

'Hi. It's me.'

'Oh, hi. Where are you?' *She sounded beautiful.*

'At the Hospitality Inn.'

She laughed. 'Yeah, I thought you might be late. I watched Ricky's fight on telly. I could see you sitting at the ringside. He must be walking on air.'

'I won't be able to see you tonight.'

'Why not?' Her voice changed. 'Is something wrong?'

'I'll tell you tomorrow. I'll meet you for lunch or something.'

'For lunch? What d'you mean?'

'I'll tell you tomorrow.'

'Billy, you're getting me scared. Something's wrong, isn't it? I can tell by your voice.'

'What?' I said dully.

'There's something wrong. Isn't there?'

I was going to lie, but lying was making me tired. 'Yeah. Everything's wrong.' *It always is.*

She started to cry. 'You're scaring me. I thought you loved me.'

I do. 'I'll talk to you tomorrow.'

It was raining outside. I walked over to the West End and just wandered around for a while. I didn't see many people. It felt good to be alone in the rainy darkness and walk past the silent houses. The rain and the darkness made the night safe and anonymous, and that was good. Sometimes you can only think about yourself properly if you're alone.

Finally, I went home. I hadn't been in the flat for quite a while and it was strange. Karen didn't wake when I went into the bedroom. There was a poster on the wall above the bed, a birthday present from Kerry.

I undressed and got into bed. Karen put an arm round me and murmured, 'You're cold.' I kissed her on the nose.

The mattress was firm and comfortable. I recalled the sagging antique I'd slept on in Edinburgh. It was daylight and it was still raining outside and Karen's nakedness was wrapped round mine. I turned in her embrace and lay with my back to her.

Ricky defends the title soon.

A NOTE ON THE AUTHOR

Barry Graham was born in Glasgow and is in his mid-twenties. He has had a variety of occupations, including professional boxing and journalism, and for a year was deputy editor of Glasgow's *Inside Out* magazine.

He moved to Edinburgh in 1988, after writing his first novel, *Of Darkness and Light*, which was published the following year. He spent six months in Inverness, didn't like it, went back to Edinburgh and has been there since.

Sections of his books have been dramatised by the Royal Lyceum Theatre in Edinburgh, and he is the founder of the Garret Party, the loose group of Scottish underground writers and musicians. He organised and took part in the 'Garret Garden Party', the astonishing open-air reading in an Edinburgh park.

Barry Graham writes prose, drama and poetry, and is presently at work on a third novel.